Indiscretions

By Cruise
(Debbie Bathurst)

1

Copyright © 2002 by Cruise

ISBN   0-9726444-8-2

First Printing 2003
Cover art and design by:
Monica Rivera (MRWarrior)

Published by:
Dare 2 Dream Publishing
A Division of Limitless Corporation
Lexington, South Carolina 29073

Find us on the World Wide Web
http://www.limitlessd2d.net

Printed in the United States of America by
Axess Purchasing Solutions
PO Box 500835
Atlanta, GA 31150

Acknowledgements

Special Thanks:

To my lovely partner Monica for her help with editing, the artwork for the book and for her unwavering love and support with my writing passion. You're the best!

To Stoley for all of your support and for being such a wonderful friend.

To the wonderful web sites that host my stories: Forevaxena, Beyond Uber, The Royal Academy of Bards, The Athenaeum, The Ultimate Fan Fiction Directory, Casa Uber, Pasha's Fan Fiction Obsessions, Shawdofen's Xena: Warrior Princess Fan Fiction Index, and The Uber Adobe. I appreciate all of your hard work and support.

An extra special thanks to the readers who have supported my writing and made my dream of being published a reality.

To Sam and Anne for being such great publishers and for taking a chance on me!

I

Rayne rushed into the building nervously wondering why the director called an important meeting with her. She worried that she might have done something inappropriate or wrong during her last assignment, from the tone of his voice on the phone when he called the meeting. She couldn't imagine what she could have done, seeing as how there were no problems during the assignment. *'Calm yourself down Rayne it's probably just a formality.'* She thought, trying to calm her nerves as she approached the secretary's desk. "Agent Donovan reporting for my meeting with Director Bailey." Rayne announced to the secretary, stoically standing in front of the attractive secretary.

"I'll tell him you're here Agent Donovan." She answered cheerfully with a smile, gazing up into Rayne's piercing blue eyes and phoned the director to inform him his next appointment was waiting for him. "He'll be with you in a moment." She announced and watched Rayne pace nervously about the waiting room.

Rayne was dressed in a black blazer, black long sleeved mock turtleneck shirt and black neatly pressed black 'Docker' pants. She checked her clothing over to make sure there was no lint present that might embarrass her during her meeting with the head honcho.

The secretary stole glances of the attractive tall, tanned, muscular woman with shoulder length black hair and chuckled as she watched her check her clothing over nervously. The phone buzzed and she answered it, and then hung the phone up, looking to Rayne. "Director Bailey will see you now." The woman replied with a sultry smile, obviously smitten with Rayne.

"Aah, thanks." Rayne stammered nervously and headed for the door.

Rayne had worked for the Secret Service for over five years and had never been called into the director's office for such a formal meeting. He had always been very casual with his meetings and from the tone of his voice when he called this one it seemed very serious. She took a deep breath before entering his office and approached the director's desk and stood before him. "Agent Donovan reporting as asked sir." Rayne announced as she stood at attention in front of the director.

"Rayne, please. You don't have to be so formal. Take a seat and breathe please." He answered with a chuckle, watching Rayne breathe a sigh of relief and sit down.

'Well, so far so good. If he were pissed at me he would have already chewed me out.' Rayne thought and nervously tapped her fingers on the chair handles. "Is there a problem sir?" Rayne asked nervously, her curiosity was killing her and she couldn't wait any longer to find out what was going on.

"Yes there is Agent." He answered and looked into a folder on his desk.

"Sir?" Rayne questioned, swallowing the lump in her throat.

"You have been working entirely too much and too far away." He answered with a smile. "That's why I called you in here today to give you a different assignment than you're usual covert operations."

"Aah okay." Rayne stammered wondering what kind of an assignment she would be getting next.

He handed her the folder he had on his desk. "This is your next assignment. Protecting this prominent figure." He explained as Rayne looked over the folder and the expression on her face turned to anger.

"Sorry sir. This isn't protection it's torture and I can't accept this assignment, sir." Rayne angrily refused, returning the folder to him and stood up to calm her nerves.

"I'm sorry Rayne there is no negotiation with this one. You have to take this assignment. You can't turn it down." He ordered demandingly and sat back in his chair, looking up at his tall agent.

"Sir, with all due respect. What in the hell did I do wrong to deserve this assignment?" She asked agitatedly and wiped the sweat off her brow as old feelings of betrayal that she thought she had buried crept back in.

"You're my top agent and highly decorated. Just the person for this assignment whether you like it or not." He explained unwaveringly and leaned forward in his chair.

"Then I quit sir." Rayne told him, laying her badge and gun on his desk and turned towards the door.

"Rayne, someone is going to kidnap her and maybe worse... kill her."

'Damn it Rayne! Just walk out the door. Why should it matter to you after what she did to you?' She inwardly questioned and hung her head defeated, wishing she wasn't doing what she was about to do. She turned back to the director and retrieved her gun and badge from his desk.

"I see you still care." He commented, happy that Rayne reconsidered, knowing the past relationship she had with the person requiring the protection.

"Unfortunately." Rayne answered aggravated with herself for not just walking out, but she knew no matter what happened between her and the person she was to protect she did still care enough to not want that kind of a demise for her. "Give me the specs on the case sir." Rayne asked as she holstered her gun and put her badge away.

7

"She has become a very popular actress of late and considering her father is a high profile Congressman her life has been placed in danger. We think it is someone within her group of

handlers and we need you there undercover to protect her. I personally wanted you to handle this because, I fear one of our agents may be involved in the conspiracy as well." He explained, not pleased with the fact that one of his own could be criminally involved.

"Why would they want to do anything to her?" Rayne asked confused.

"To get to her father and influence his vote regarding his stance with the war in Kosovo. Seems that he will be the deciding factor as to whether our troops will be pulled out in that region and there are many people who don't want our influence there. So, they figure by kidnapping his daughter they will have leverage to get the vote swayed in their favor."

"Why me though? There are other top agents who could handle this case." Rayne asked perplexed.

"Because you two were once together and the inside perpetrators won't suspect anything by you being there. They will think there has been reconciliation between the two of you. Besides, the Congressman specifically asked for you to protect his daughter. Seems he likes you." The director answered sarcastically and grinned.

Rayne chuckled and shook her head in disbelief. "Unbelievable." She commented softly and looked back up at her director. "Does she know what's going on?"

"Yes, but not about you, yet. She's in the next room being briefed on how everything is to be handled from now on. You'll be assigned to her until after Congress meets and places their votes in a week. Come on let's head in there."

8

"Might as well get it over with." Rayne suggested with agitation and hesitation for not wanting to face her. *'How bad could a week be?'* Rayne wondered inwardly, but she already knew the answer to her question. *'Pure hell, what I do for my country!'* Rayne commented, shaking her head in disbelief as to how her life just took a dramatic change for the worse.

The Director and Rayne headed towards the room to discuss the plans with the woman. Rayne wished she could be anywhere but here at this moment, and she was kicking herself for not walking out the door when she had the chance. It took her nearly six months to bury her feelings towards her former lover, deep enough to where she could function without wanting to kill someone.

Every negative thought she had then or the feelings of complete devastation that comes about when someone you loved so much could betray you in such a way, all came rushing back. *'I guess I didn't bury them deep enough.'* Rayne inwardly realized and followed the director who entered the room.

The blond woman sat talking with another agent as Rayne stepped into the room unnoticed. Her striking appearance, as usual, took Rayne's breath away when she glanced over at her. Rayne inhaled deeply to calm her racing heart and desire to ream the woman a new butt hole for what she had done to her six months ago. The woman she once loved more than life itself had now become someone she hated. *'I guess I don't hate her as much as I thought if I'm standing here willing to protect her with me life. Nah, it's hate, but I'm just a glutton for punishment.'* Rayne reasoned as the blonde turned to see the director and Rayne standing just beyond her boss.

Her face lit up at the sight of Rayne and her emerald green eyes met angered blues. Tears welled in her eyes as she stood and approached Rayne. "Rayne, you came." She replied softly and appreciatively, rushing over to engulf her former lover in a tight hug. Rayne always loved how this woman felt in her arms and

9

those feelings rushed back as she held her. There was a part of her that wanted to hold her and tell her all was forgiven, but she couldn't do it. "I knew you would come back one day." She whispered in Rayne's ear. Rayne put her hands on the woman's arms to remove them from their tight grip and stepped back.

"I didn't come back willingly Lark, it's my job. Nothing more." Rayne's contempt with the woman was evident with her answer as her blue eyes glared into greens.

Lark searched Rayne's blues for validity of her last statement, and found nothing but hate in them. "Silly me to have thought something else." She whispered disappointed as Rayne let her hands go.

"Yes it was." Rayne coldly answered and stepped away from the shorter blonde with obvious disdain.

The director noticed the unpleasantness of the situation and decided to change the subject. "Okay now, if you are asked by reporters about the two of you being seen together again, you are to tell them there has been a reconciliation and you're both overly ecstatic about it.

"Oh, yeah. Can't you see it all over my face?" Rayne sarcastically retorted, agitated by the situation and glanced over at Lark to see her reaction of hurt.

"Rayne, for this to work this has to be believable. So, that means in public you are to exude your normal show of affection as you did before and look happy to be back in each other's lives." Director Bailey ordered, slightly agitated with her attitude. "Explain that you have given up your job as the Congressman's aide which was your cover before to concentrate on your relationship with Lark and, that you'll be assuming duties as her personal assistant."

"You've got to be kidding me! You mean to tell me I have to make it look like I'm giving up everything for her?" Rayne asked with anger in her voice and pointed at the blonde.

"That's right. The press will eat it up as will her public." The director answered.

"I swear this is one bad fucking nightmare!" Rayne answered in disgust and ran her hand through her raven hair frustrated.

"Rayne all you have to do is pretend. This is not real." The director explained.

"She's better at that than me seeing as how she pretended to love me and now I have to bow down to her in public? Give me a break!" Rayne angrily answered and stormed out of the room.

"Rayne! Wait please!" Lark pleaded and exited the room as the taller woman headed down the hall.

'Unbelievable! I'm the jilted lover here and now I'm made out to look like the one who was the cause of the break up.' Rayne thought with fiery blue eyes as she approached the soda machine and put a dollar in for a Dr. Pepper, which didn't come out. "Fucking machine!" Rayne shouted aggravated, and shook the machine then pounded on it.

"Rayne, please I need your help." Lark pleaded with Rayne as she approached.

"Find someone else to walk all over like a doormat. Been there done that and hated it." Rayne answered with mounting agitation as she shook the machine.

"Rayne, I'm sorry I hurt you the way I did."

Rayne became enraged. "Hurt me Lark? Hurt me? You devastated me you fucking bitch!" Rayne yelled and pounded on the soda machine to take out her frustrations.

11

"Rayne, please stop. I'll get the soda out." Lark suggested and offered with tears in her eyes from Rayne's comments. She grabbed Rayne's hands to make her stop, which calmed Rayne's temper. Rayne remembered how Lark was able to calm her with the touch of her hand and didn't want to feel that, and jerked her hands away from her.

Lark repositioned the dollar, which had fallen out unseen by Rayne because of her temper tantrum and pushed the button for a Dr. Pepper, which promptly dropped out of the machine. She handed it to Rayne who snatched it out of her hand. "Oh, look here. Lark to the rescue." Rayne replied sarcastically. "Where were you a few months ago when I needed you?" Rayne asked with hate in her eyes.

"Rayne, I know I wasn't there for you and I regret that. I can only hope that you can put your feelings of hate aside long enough to get through this whole escapade that's happening in my life.

"Of course Lark, anything for you isn't that right?" Rayne angrily asked and stormed off.

"What is the living arrangements sir?" Rayne asked upon entering the room, knowing she wasn't going to like the answer he was about to give her.

"We've set up a new condo for her to live in, which will be free of bugs and hidden cameras. You'll stay there with her of course." He answered with a smile to calm the tension he saw in Rayne's blue eyes.

"I have to stop by my apartment to pick up some of my clothes and personal items sir." Rayne explained as she drained the rest of her Dr. Pepper and trashed the can.

"No problem, her limo will follow you to your apartment and then take the both of you to her new condo. The limo is in the garage basement and no one will know the two of you have been here as long as you take the secret passage out." He explained and looked at his top agent with worry. "You going to be okay?"

"Who the hell knows?" Rayne answered agitated by the whole ordeal and exited the office to see Lark waiting in the hallway for her. "I was hoping this was all a nightmare, but I guess not since you're still here." Rayne replied disgustedly as she looked at the attractive blonde.

"Are you ever going to forgive me?" Lark asked and grabbed Rayne's arm to stop her.

Rayne looked down at the hand that held her arm and looked up at Lark with stormy blue eyes. "Never!" Rayne exclaimed with disdain and anger. She jerked her arm away from Lark and headed down the hall towards the elevator followed by an obviously upset blonde.

'I guess I deserve the treatment I'm receiving from Rayne, but it still hurts to see how much she hates me. I never thought I would ever see the stranger in her eyes, but that's exactly what I see and I'm the cause of everything.' Lark thought with regret and kept her head down to avoid looking at Rayne as she stepped onto the elevator.

The two never spoke a word throughout the elevator ride. They reached the basement and Rayne headed straight for the limo with Lark following behind. "Dude! No way! I'm so psyched you'll be on this assignment too!" Rayne replied with excitement and a smile as she approached the agent posing as the limo driver.

"I know it's great!" The attractive dirty blonde answered and hugged Rayne.

"Danielle, how the hell have you been? I haven't seen you for a few weeks." Rayne excitedly asked and stood close to the other agent with her hand still resting on the woman's waist. She was happy Danielle had this assignment as she trusted her completely and knew it would make her job easier having her there.

Lark stood watching jealously by the limo and tried not to make it obvious that she was staring. She wished she could hear their conversation, but she wasn't close enough.

"I've been doing great Rayne. How about you?"

"Could be better and as soon as I finish this babysitting mission it will be a hell of a lot better!" Rayne commented loathingly at her latest assignment and glanced over her shoulder at Lark for Danielle to get her drift.

"Aah isn't that Lark Morgan, the actress?" She asked and tried to catch a better glimpse of the woman.

"The one and only. She's my ex." Rayne dryly commented.

"Ah-ha. Now, I see why you hate this assignment. I'm sorry to hear you two are no longer together. I remember you telling me about her during our various assignments. Hang in there buddy." Danielle answered with a smile and rubbed Rayne's arm for comfort as the pair made their way to the limo. Rayne knew their interaction was killing Lark, but she didn't care. She didn't mind letting Lark believe something romantic was going on between her and Danielle despite the fact that they were just good friends.

Lark climbed in the back followed by Rayne and each sat at opposite ends of the seat looking out the windows. *'It shouldn't bother me that she has found another, but it does because I still love her. I was such an ass to do what I did and drive her out of my life.'* Lark inwardly admonished and turned to look at Rayne who was in deep thought as she looked out the window.

"Aah is she a girlfriend or just a lover?" Lark asked nervously and wondered why she asked that question.

14

Rayne turned and looked at Lark with stormy blue eyes. "That's none of your business." She snapped and looked back out the window.

Lark turned her head towards the window and looked out as tears streamed down her face. She wondered if Rayne would ever forgive her for her indiscretions and hoped that one-day she would. She still loved Rayne with all her heart despite the fact that she turned to another, and she desperately wanted Rayne back. She believed that Rayne is her soul mate and they were meant to be together. She wished she could take back what happened six months ago.

The limo pulled up in front of Rayne's apartment building and Rayne stepped out first to check the area before Lark exited the limo. They headed towards the entrance of the building and Rayne stayed close to Lark's side as they approached the gate and held it open for her playing the part of her girlfriend well in case they were being watched.

They entered the apartment and Lark checked the spacious place out. "This is a really nice place Rayne." She cordially commented and sat on the couch.

Rayne entered the living room. "What type of engagements do you have this week that we'll have to be attending?" Rayne asked, ignoring Lark's comment.

"Hmmm, three movie premiere's and one award show." Lark answered as she thought about what appointments she had scheduled for the week.

Rayne headed into the bedroom and began to pack clothes that she would need for the week. Rayne hurried to pack her bag as Lark entered the bedroom. "Do you need any help?" She offered as Rayne ignored her while she continued to pack. "Look Rayne. I know this is very difficult for you, but don't you think it would be easier if it was more of a civil environment?" Lark asked hoping Rayne would reconsider her demeanor.

15

"Easier for who? You? Why should I be civil to you Lark? What reason would I have to do that?" Rayne sarcastically and angrily asked staring the shorter woman down.

"Because you loved me at one time. Isn't that reason enough?" Lark shot back.

"NO, it's not enough Lark. Key word here is I loved you at one time, no more. So, to answer you're question about me being civil. No, I can't." Rayne answered matter of fact as she closed her travel bag and headed into the other room to gather her paperwork, laptop computer and equipment to check for hidden cameras and bugs.

"Fair enough." Lark answered dejectedly and entered the living room as Rayne threw her bags over her shoulder and headed toward the door.

Rayne and Lark made their way to the limo with Rayne keeping Lark close to her side and surveyed the area for anything out of the ordinary as Lark climbed into the limo. Danielle put the limo in gear and headed off towards Lark's new condo. The ride was quiet until the limo pulled up in front of Lark's condo to find a crowd of photographers waiting for her. "Bite me!" Rayne exclaimed as she looked out at the people waiting for them. "How the hell did they know we would be here?" Rayne exclaimed with disbelief.

"You should know by now that they know more than the damn government when it comes to finding people for a picture." Lark answered with regret that she had to face the paparazzi. "Are you ready for this Rayne?" Lark asked with concern and looked over at the attractive Secret Service agent who made her heart melt every time she looked at her.

"As ready as I'm ever going to be I guess. Stay very close to me. Do you understand?" Rayne firmly ordered to get her point across to Lark that she was serious.

16

'How can she ask that question when she knows I love to be close to her, but she won't allow that anymore.' Lark thought before responding, "I understand completely."

"Okay Danielle. Bring my luggage and laptop in behind us." Rayne ordered as Danielle nodded in agreement to confirm the orders. "Let's get going then." Rayne answered with a deep sigh as she opened the door and threw her equipment bag over her shoulder.

"Rayne! Are you and Lark back together?" A reporter shouted.

"Rayne! What brings you back?" Another asked.

Rayne ignored the reporters' questions as she held the door open for Lark to step out of the limo. "Hey, fellas back it up so we can get out!" Rayne agitatedly told them after the door to the limo slammed into her back when the photographers shoved their way closer for a picture. Rayne shoved the door back into them and held her hand out for Lark to help her exit the limo as she braced the door against her to keep it from closing again.

Lark stood and looked up as emerald green eyes met piercing blues. Lark swore she saw a glimmer of hope for the two of them in Rayne's eyes and hesitated momentarily to stare into those sexy blue eyes longer. The lingering stare of Lark's made Rayne feel uncomfortable and she broke the look when she stepped back for Lark to step away from the car.

"Lark, what's the story?" One photographer shouted.

"What does it look like?" Lark answered with a mischievous smile as Rayne put her arm around Lark to keep up the façade. She pulled her close to while she scanned the crowd for anything out of the ordinary as did Danielle who moved to the back of the limo to get the luggage. The gesture sent a rush of warmth throughout

17

Lark and her heart skipped a beat as she enjoyed feeling so close to Rayne.

"It looks like you two are back together." Someone shouted.

"Hey, give him all the money in Fort Knox for figuring out the best kept secret first." Rayne replied sarcastically as Lark laughed along with the other photographers. Rayne guided Lark through the crowd towards the entrance to the building.

"Are you two happy?" Someone shouted as the pair turned back to face the questioner.

"Very happy, thanks." Lark answered with a smile, leaning up and kissing Rayne on the cheek.

"Ecstatic!" Rayne added with a strained smile to hide her anger for what Lark just did to her. She hurried Lark up to the door and held it open for her to enter the heavily guarded building.

The security guards sat in awe as the famous, beautiful blonde entered the building. "Close your mouth boys or flies will collect in there. She's with me so eat your heart out." Rayne laughed with a wink as the pair made their way into the elevator arm and arm despite the fact that inwardly Rayne was seething with anger for having to pretend like they were in love again.

As soon as the doors closed to the elevator Rayne moved away from Lark as quickly as possible. Lark was disappointed, as it felt so right to have Rayne's arm around her. Rayne's touch always told her just how much she loved her and Lark still felt it from her. *'Is it just that I want to feel that or does she still love me despite all her hate for me. Maybe, I can only hope.'* Lark thought and stole a quick glance of Rayne who remained silent as she looked through her bag. Lark loved to look at Rayne. Hell, who wouldn't? She was gorgeous! Tall, dark, muscular, with exquisitely beautiful blue eyes that Lark lost herself in, she had a sexy yet, cocky demeanor about her that attracted Lark to Rayne in the first place, and a wonderful sense of humor despite the latter being hidden from all her hate.

Lark felt extremely guilty for what she had done to Rayne. All of Rayne's wonderful traits to her personality were gone and replaced by disdain and hate caused by her betrayal. What she saw now was just a stoic Secrete Service Agent who was cut and dry, all business. Well, other than the outburst of anger she inflicted on Lark. *'I know I saw a glimmer of hope in those sexy blue eyes. Maybe if we talk and hash everything out we might have a chance of reconciliation. A true one not a manufactured one.'* Lark thought hopeful.

"Hey, Lark snap out of La La land!" Rayne commented sarcastically as Lark looked up at her confused.

"Huh? What?" Lark asked, snapped out of her thoughts that she lost herself in.

"This is your floor. Let's go." Rayne retorted curtly as she walked off the elevator and headed to the apartment number listed on the file her director had given her.

"Oh, yeah. Okay." Lark stammered nervously and followed Rayne down the hall to her new condo.

Rayne noticed the door was opened a crack and heard voices inside the apartment. She pushed Lark behind her and leaned up against the wall out of sight to see if she could decipher what the voices were saying, opening her jacket and putting her hand on her gun just in case.

Lark's heart raced nervously as she stood behind Rayne and put her hand on Rayne's waist to feel more at ease by making a connection with her. Rayne glanced over her shoulder at Lark when she felt her hand on her waist and turned back listening to the conversation. Rayne recognized the familiar voice as being Danny's, Lark's accountant. Rayne leaned her head against the wall and let out a sigh of relief or was it a sigh of angst that she was going into the frying pan? She thought the reporters outside were bad. These people are going to be worse. Asking far too many personal questions and these are the one's she really has to convince that the whole set up isn't a sham. Lark leaned closer to Rayne and whispered in her ear. "What is going on?"

Rayne felt Lark's breath on her neck, which, much to her surprise excited her. She looked at Lark and caught herself staring into Lark's green eyes a little longer than what she had wanted to do. "Aah, its Danny and the rest of your group." Rayne stammered and tried to calm her excitement.

"Whew! I was worried." Lark answered relieved.

"Remember, one of these people are in on the whole thing Lark. Don't be so quick to be so trusting of them." Rayne sternly reminded her, moving away from the wall and laced her fingers around Larks, which took Lark's breath away momentarily from her touch.

Rayne led her into the apartment and everyone was at first shocked to see Rayne, but then was ecstatic to see the two of them back together. Rayne was greeted by Danny, Lark's accountant; Elaine, her agent; Frank, her lawyer; and Hazel her longtime maid/cook/jack of all trades. One other person approached that Rayne had never met before.

"Ah Rayne this is my personal trainer Kim. Kim, this is the love of my life, meet Rayne." Lark introduced them with Rayne squeezing her hand tightly at Lark's comment to let her know that she didn't particularly like what she said about her being the love of her life.

"Hello Kim it's a pleasure to meet you." Rayne greeted as she held her hand out to shake the woman's hand, and tried to be as cordial as possible considering she was sweating bullets from feeling so uncomfortable. The uncomfortable feelings she had when they broke up were consuming her and she hated being back in that environment.

"Same here." Kim answered looking Rayne over with a cautious eye.

Rayne took in some deep breaths and stood in behind Lark and wrapped her arms around the smaller woman. "Could we have some privacy to get caught up with one another? I've been away a very long time." Rayne asked with a suggestive smile on her face and leaned her chin against Lark's shoulder. Rayne just didn't want to deal with the onslaught of all the questions she knew she was about to be hit with, and figured this was a good way out of them for the time being.

Lark reveled in how close Rayne was to her and absolutely loved the feeling of her arms wrapped around her. She didn't want it to end and hoped everyone would take their time leaving so she could stay in that position. She new the second the door closed Rayne would release her. *'How could I have been such an idiot to have hurt this woman that I love more than life itself the way that I did?'* Lark inwardly questioned and watched the last person walk past her knowing her pleasure was about to end.

As the door closed Rayne let go of Lark and pushed away from her. "Rayne, what the hell was up with...?" Lark tried to finish her sentence but was cut off by a hand to the mouth as she looked into Rayne's blues with bewilderment.

Rayne slowly moved towards Lark's ear and her heart raced with anticipation that Rayne would kiss her neck like she used to. "Follow my lead with idle chit chat, understood." Rayne whispered impersonally and leaned back to look at Lark who was obviously disappointed. She nodded in agreement that she would, watching Rayne open her equipment bag and remove some equipment that would detect if the condo had been bugged. "So, what do you want to eat?" Rayne asked as she turned the machine on and scanned the living room.

"How about you?" Lark answered mischievously hoping she could trigger a more receptive response out of Rayne than the usual one of disgust.

Rayne snapped her head around with a cross look on her face and pointed at Lark to let her know she wasn't pleased with the comment. "Well, you'll have to wait on that one now won't you?" Rayne answered teasingly to keep up the charade in case the place was bugged from one of Lark's employees who had been in the condo.

"I look forward to it, but until then how about if we order Chinese?" Lark suggested with a defiant look on her face to let Rayne know she was tired of her gruffness.

Rayne scanned the living room, kitchen and phone's finding no bugs. "Sure, go ahead and order for us." Rayne suggested and headed into the bedroom to check the rest of the condo, which she found to be free of any bugs or hidden cameras.

Rayne entered the living room while Lark ordered Chinese for them as someone knocked. Rayne opened the door to find Danielle standing there with Rayne's bags. "Hey! Thanks I appreciate it." She greeted with a smile and it was obvious that this woman put Rayne in a better mood than Lark does. Lark looked on with obvious jealousy at the pair's interaction. She knew she was the one who brought all of this on, but she still loved Rayne and desperately wanted her back. This woman was treading on her territory and she despised it.

"No problem, other than almost having to fire my gun to get through the crowd." Danielle answered with a laugh, which was shared by Rayne. "I have a place here and I'm heading off to ditch the limo so, no one will notice me coming back. If you two have to go out call me and I'll double back for the limo. Also, if you need my assistance if anything goes down okay? Here's the new number." She explained and handed Rayne her business card with the number on it.

"Great, thanks for your help Danielle." Rayne smiled appreciatively, watching the attractive agent walk away and closed the door after she was out of sight.

"Are you just doing that to piss me off?" Lark angrily asked.

"Is it working?" Rayne sarcastically asked and grinned.

"Do you have to be such a bitch?" Lark asked in a raised tone.

"Did you have to be six months ago?" Rayne snapped in a low assertive voice, watching Lark who shook her head in disgust and stormed out of the room, slamming the bedroom door.

Rayne sat on the couch and wondered just what the hell she was doing. Lark was driving her crazy! It had been easier when she was out of the state and away from Lark since their breakup. Right now, she wished she were anywhere but there. She grabbed some Advil and downed the pills with water to take care of her pounding headache. She sat back on the couch and looked at some of the things Lark's entourage had brought there for her. She looked at the crystal Dolphin statue and smiled fondly at the memory of when she gave that to Lark. She gave it to her for her birthday and knew Lark would love it, as she was so enamored with Dolphins. She remembered the look of excitement, happiness and love for her that Lark expressed to her when she opened the present. Rayne ran an absent hand through her raven hair. *'What are you doing remembering crap like that Rayne? What do you think, that you're still in love with her?'* She inwardly questioned, conflicted from her thoughts and hoped it wasn't the latter.

When they broke up she swore she would never love or give her heart to another like did with Lark, who ripped it away from her. Nope, she couldn't go through that and definitely didn't want to do it again with Lark no matter how many old, fond memories were dredged up thinking, *'Once a cheater always a cheater.'* with anger consuming her once again at the thought of how Lark had cheated on her, them, their love for one another. She was unable to

23

handle the thoughts and pushed them to that secret place she had deep inside so, she could cope with the love she lost.

Rayne leaned her aching head against the back of the couch and closed her eyes trying to figure out just how one person's life could become so hellish. She put her hands over her eyes and drifted off to sleep.

The visions in her dreams were back again. She thought she had gotten rid of the same damn dream she had over and over again, but she was wrong. It was the dream of her walking into the house with a bouquet of red roses and a huge mischievous smile on her face, knowing she was home from her assignment early to surprise Lark. *'She couldn't wait to see the love of her life and hold her in her arms'*, she happily thought as she quietly walked down the hall and opened the door to complete devastation.

Rayne jumped out of her sleep from the incessant knocking on the door that she faintly heard. She realized that was no dream, it was reality and was glad she was awake and didn't have to see that again. She opened the door to find the deliveryman waiting impatiently with their food. "Aah sorry, here." Rayne stammered, trying to wake from her slumber and handed him some money to cover the bill plus a hefty tip.

"Hey, thanks!" He answered excitedly and walked off.

Rayne shut the door and put the food down on the counter. She searched the cupboards for plates and yelled for Lark to come and get it. "I'm already here." Lark answered with a laugh as she entered the kitchen eagerly awaiting the food.

A smile crept on Rayne's face from the fact that Lark was standing behind her and that she just knew Lark had food radar that went off when anything edible was present. Rayne hid the smile on her face and kept her back turned to Lark while pouring some fried rice out on her plate. She took her plate with the utensils, a Dr. Pepper and sat down at the table to eat her meal.

Lark piled the Chinese food on her plate and headed over towards the sliding glass door. "Damn, I can't handle all this stuff and open the door." She sighed, frustrated.

"Lark, get away from the window." Rayne sternly ordered when she looked up to see what Lark was doing.

"Why?" Lark asked confused.

"Just do as I say." Rayne angrily answered and looked back down at her plate.

"No, not until you tell me why." Lark defiantly refused, glaringly staring at Rayne.

Rayne's anger inside began to boil and she dropped her fork on the table, and then stood up with a look of disdain on her face. She moved towards Lark and brushed past her to close the mini-blinds above the sliding glass doors. "You just love to piss me off don't you?" Rayne asked agitated with the blonde and stood face to face with her.

"What is the big deal to sit out on the balcony?"

"You'd be an easy target for a sniper Lark that's why." Rayne angrily informed her and walked back to the table, sitting down to finish her meal.

"Would that bother you Rayne if a sniper took a shot at me?" Lark asked hoping she would get a caring response out of Rayne.

"Yes, because they would kill you and I've never had anyone that I have protected get killed." Rayne answered completely disinterested in playing Lark's game, and filled her mouth with a forkful of rice.

"So, that's all I mean to you is part of one of your statistics for work that you haven't lost someone yet?" Lark asked, upset by her comment.

"Yep." Rayne answered without concern and continued to eat, never looking up at Lark.

"Great, just great!" Lark angrily shouted and stormed off into her bedroom.

Rayne dropped her fork agitated and was no longer hungry. Lark frustrated the hell out of her and she wondered if it was because she hated her so much or because she still loved her. It was easier for her to hate Lark, so she went with that.

Rayne contacted her director regarding air and hotel arrangements for their trip to California for one of the many movie premiere's Lark had to attend starting the next day. He informed her of the afternoon flight scheduled and the itinerary for her getting Lark to the airport and on the plane safely.

Rayne finished her plans for the trip and did a quick check of the locks and security alarm to make sure the condo was secured before bed. She checked the other rooms and headed down the hall to Lark's bedroom, which was very silent other than the static sound coming from the TV. She reached for the door and pulled back reluctantly. She was afraid of what she might find behind the door. *'Get a grip Rayne. You two are the only one's in the condo.'* She reminded and cracked the door to find Lark sound asleep on the bed.

She entered the room and checked the windows to make sure they were secure, and shut off the TV before stealing a glance of the beautiful sleeping blonde. It was beyond her how the woman she loved with every ounce of her being could hurt her as much as she did and it baffled her even more why she cared enough to take this assignment considering the pain she went through from Lark's actions. She pulled the covers up on her and gazed upon her; momentarily reveling in how peaceful she looked sleeping, not to mention her unassuming beauty that highlighted her fine features. This interaction was so familiar to her that she caught herself leaning down to lightly kiss Lark's forehead, but stopped when

26

she realized what she was about to do. She couldn't allow herself to get drawn in by her and shut the light off then left the room to sleep on the couch.

The next morning Rayne had a meeting with Lark's staff explaining that she was Lark's new personal assistant and that she would make all the arrangements for any appearances. She also instructed the staff that she and Lark would be the only people privy to the travel plans for her safety. She would give them a time frame for traveling and within it they would leave for their destination at the last minute. Lark's staff was put off, but they knew it was best for her. Rayne had her suspicions as to which person the insider was and had asked her director to form a file for each individual so she could study them and try to figure out who would gain the most from betraying Lark.

Rayne's plans worked to perfection and they arrived in California in the early evening. Rayne protectively kept Lark close as they approached the front desk clerk to check in at the hotel. "Hello, I'm Rayne Donovan and I have reservations for this evening."

"Oh, yes Miss Donovan. Here is your key to the presidential suite." The clerk informed Rayne as Lark looked on with obvious enjoyment that they would be staying in the most expensive suite in the hotel.

"There's been a change in plans. Our staff will take the presidential suite and we will take one of your regular suites." Rayne informed the confused clerk.

"Aah okay let me get the key." She stammered nervously as Lark rolled her eyes disappointed that they would not be staying in the presidential suite.

Rayne handed the staff the key to their suite and instructed the staff to call on her cell phone if they needed either of them. The group left the lobby and headed off to their suite as the clerk returned with a key to a different suite.

"Here you go." She replied with a smile and handed Rayne the key.

"Thank you." Rayne answered with a smile, then leaned down and picked up her bag. "Let's go." She told Lark who looked at her disgusted.

They stood on the elevator silent as usual and Lark fumed at the change of rooms as Rayne stood inwardly laughing, knowing Lark loved to travel first class and this was just killing her. Rayne spent the next few hours explaining to Lark the different itinerary's consisting of travel plans of how they would accomplish getting her to the assorted appearances safely. Lark was happy that they actually had a civil conversation without fighting throughout the entire briefing. She said goodnight and headed off to bed as Rayne laid on the couch studying over the information her boss sent her regarding Lark's employees. She put that away and pulled out the story she had written to proofread it and fell asleep after only doing a few pages.

Lark woke in the early morning hours and noticed all the lights were still on in the living room of the suite and went out to see what Rayne was doing. She saw that Rayne was sound asleep and her tall body was scrunched up on the very small couch she laid on. Rayne's arms were crossed over her chest and looked as though she was cold from the air conditioning blowing down on her so Lark retrieved a blanket to cover her. Lark saw the papers on the ground and picked them up to move them. She glanced down and noticed the title of the paper and looked at Rayne to make sure she wasn't awake. She looked back at the paper titled "My lost love" and the author read "By Rayne". She read a few paragraphs and the parallels between their relationship and the fictitious one in the paper was undeniable. Rayne was writing a story of their relationship together. She looked down at Rayne who still slept peacefully and returned to her reading. She read about the character that was Rayne and how much pain they felt over the breakup and how much the character still loved the beautiful blonde in the story as she was described. Lark smiled and realized that maybe there was hope for them yet. She leaned down and covered the alluring woman she still loved more than life itself. She lovingly smiled and moved her hand up towards Rayne's face to caress it and was grabbed tightly around the wrist when Rayne felt a presence standing next to her. Lark dropped to her knees in pain as Rayne opened her blue eyes to see it was Lark.

"What the hell are you doing?" Rayne asked annoyed with Lark and edgy that she might have hurt her.

"I was just covering you up with a blanket, you looked cold." Lark apprehensively answered and struggled to loosen Rayne's grip.

Rayne looked into Lark's green eyes and saw overwhelming fear. "Did you think I would hurt you Lark?" Rayne asked surprised that Lark would feel that way.

"I wasn't sure Rayne." Lark tentatively answered and looked down at the ground sad and unsure.

Rayne was taken off guard by Lark's hesitation and her gesture of kindness. The green eyes she stared into mesmerized her and she pushed an errant strand of long blond hair off her face. She placed her hand under Lark's chin lifting it up to look at her. "I would never physically harm you Lark." Rayne sincerely admitted as Lark locked her greens with sincere blues. Lark slowly leaned toward Rayne and held her breath hoping she would allow her to kiss her. *'Should I allow her to kiss me?'* Rayne asked and watched Lark move closer to her. *'Why the hell not? I haven't had sex for a very long time and she's not bad for a roll in the hay.'* Rayne inwardly reasoned and allowed Lark to press her lips against her own.

Tears welled in Lark's eyes when Rayne allowed her to kiss her. She needed this connection to Rayne so desperately, and she was glad she was able to have it from her. Lark moved closer to Rayne who deepened the kiss. Lark broke the kiss and looked at

Rayne. "Do you really want to do this?" Lark asked hoping her answer would be yes.

II

Rayne was entranced in a sea of emerald green eyes lovingly staring at her. It took her brain a moment to register what her ears heard. She was snapped out of her trance and was instantly filled with anger. "What did you say?" Rayne asked harshly.

Lark was startled and bewildered by Rayne's terse response. It wasn't the one she expected. You know the one were Rayne sweeps her up in her arms telling her she loves her and makes mad passionate love to her for the rest of the evening, nope not that one. "Huh?" Was all Lark could muster with a confused look on her face.

"I don't stutter. What did you say?" Rayne asked with mounting agitation at Lark's evasiveness and sat up on the couch.

"Aah, I asked do you really want to do this?" Lark asked even more confused by Rayne's line of questioning.

Rayne looked down and shook her head in disbelief. "That's what I thought you said. You're freaking unbelievable Lark." Rayne answered disgusted and gathered her papers off the floor, placing them into her computer case.

"What? What did I say?" Lark asked anxiously and put her hands on Rayne's arms. She didn't want to lose the connection with her.

"Don't touch me Lark." Rayne angrily demanded and jerked her arm away.

"What did I say to upset you so much?" She asked and began to cry.

"Think about it Lark. Think back about six months ago and you'll figure it out!" Rayne angrily shouted before storming out of the room to the bathroom.

Lark sat down on the floor and hugged her knees thinking back six months ago as the tears trickled down her cheeks. She realized what she said to set Rayne's foul mood off this time. It was the same question she asked Rayne on that fateful evening and she received the same answer from Rayne, she walked out. *'How could I have been so stupid to have asked her the same thing knowing it would upset her?'* Lark asked, wondering what was wrong with her and why she continually hurt Rayne. She thought her and Rayne might be making a break through that would bring them back together, but she was wrong. Lark's tears flowed harder as she thought about how she loved Rayne so much and tried to explain things to Rayne that evening. She tried to apologize and keep her from leaving that night, but she wouldn't listen. *'Rayne has been devastated, as I would be if the same thing happened to me.'* Lark realized, remembering the hurt and pain she had seen in Rayne's blue eyes that night. *'Rayne never gave me a chance to explain. She walked out of my life for good without another word. She never came back to pick up any of her belongings and had her brother tell me she was not coming back. She just left and had her mail forwarded to an undisclosed location.'* She sadly remembered.

Rayne, Lark surmised, was able to keep her whereabouts a secret considering who she worked for and was never able to find her. Lark asked her father to help and he had no luck finding Rayne. Rayne was gone for good Lark thought at the time, until now. She knew exactly where she was, but wasn't able to do the one thing she wanted more than anything in the world, win Rayne back. Lark decided there was a reason for Rayne coming back into her life no matter how dastardly the circumstances were, but she was there and it was Lark's only chance to try and make things right again. She somehow had to get through all of Rayne's hate for her and make her fall in love with her all over again. Lark felt more confident in her intentions to win Rayne back as she headed into the bedroom to dress for her morning workout.

Rayne stood in the shower with her hands flat against the wall as the hot water beat down on her tense neck and back. She hoped the hot water would sooth the tension in her neck and shoulders. Lark had pissed her off to no end and now her body suffered for it from the stress of the situation. *'This was the worst assignment she could have possibly been assigned to.'* She thought as her anger mounted at the thought of it. She turned the dial on the shower for hotter water and told herself she should have just quit and walked out of the director's office when she had the chance. It had taken her a long time to bury her feelings of contempt for Lark to a point where she could function and now everything was coming back. She was having a hard time dealing with the feelings she had for Lark and the raw, harsh, and painful memories of what happened to them.

The same pain of betrayal that she felt before was back with a vengeance and it gripped her around the throat to a point where it felt like she couldn't breath. *'How could she have turned to another woman?'* Rayne sadly wondered as she stood up and let the water run over her head. It felt so soothing as the hot water trickled down her tense body and she felt her muscles start to slowly relax. She loved Lark with every beat of her heart and couldn't understand her indiscretions. *'Why?'* She asked and then decided she didn't want to know, just like she didn't want to know then, why? Because it would only hurt her worse and more pain was something she just didn't need right now or six months ago either.

Maybe she should find out to get closure on this so she could move on, but the thought of hearing the details of another woman making love to Lark nauseated her and gripped her heart like a vice. No, she didn't want to hear it. *'I guess I'll never have closure.'* Rayne realized and finished showering, then stepped out to dry off and start the day.

She looked at herself in the mirror and liberally applied the hair gel in her raven hair and asked, *'How do I gather the strength to get through this facade without having a breakdown?'* Discipline was the answer she came up with, *'Discipline,'* she repeated. *'Remember, they taught you that in the military and during your training with the Secret Service? So, remember it.'*

Rayne instructed her psyche, combing her hair and once finished, slipped on her robe as she headed out for her clothes.

Rayne exited the bathroom to find Lark in the middle of her workout with Kim. She casually slipped past the open door in the bedroom unnoticed by both of the women and pulled out a pair of black tightly fitting jeans, a white T-shirt and grabbed her black mid-thigh leather jacket for when they left to conceal her weapon. She finished dressing and headed out of the room to the table where Hazel had croissants, bagels and muffins laid out with freshly brewed 'African Cinnamon' flavored coffee ready for her to savor.

The coffee was her favorite and a smile slipped on her face when the aroma met her. "Hazel, I have missed you beyond belief!" She complimented with a smile after taking a sip of the tasty coffee.

"I've missed you as well Rayne." Hazel answered with a smile and a loving pat on the back. "I'm glad you're back." She admitted and leaned down, whispering in Rayne's ear before she left the room.

'I wish I was.' Rayne sarcastically thought as she munched on a blueberry muffin, also one of her favorites.

Lark, Kim and Hazel entered the room as Rayne looked over the day's itinerary she had written out. "Hello, sweetheart." Lark greeted sweetly with a smile as she leaned down and kissed Rayne's cheek. Lark took an opportunity to admire what Rayne was wearing and was quite pleased with her attire. *'Oh, she is so damn hot! She drives me insane with her sexiness.'* Lark inwardly thought appreciative of Rayne's good looks and gave Rayne a lingering look, ever so wanting to take her in the bedroom and make mad, passionate love to the sexy beast!

"Morning." Rayne flatly answered with a strained smile as she tried to keep from choking Lark from the kiss.

Everyone sat down to eat and conversed in idle chit chat as Rayne pretended to study the itinerary which she had memorized by heart so she wouldn't have to join in on the conversation when someone knocked on the door.

"I'll get it!" Rayne called out and jumped out of her seat seizing the opportunity to get away from the women, rushing to the door. She opened the door to find her brother Shayan with her two nephews Brandon and Cole standing there that surprised her.

"Auntie Rayne!" They shouted excitedly and both engulfed her in a hug when she squatted down to greet them.

"Hey, how are my two favorite guys?" She asked with a smile.

"Great!" They answered in unison. "Where's Auntie Lark?" They asked exuberantly as they looked over Rayne's shoulder for her.

"Geez, what am I? Chopped liver? You see me for not even two seconds and you already want to see Lark." Rayne teased the two as Lark stepped into the room.

"Auntie Lark!" They shouted released their hold on Rayne, running to hug her.

Rayne watched the greeting with an adoring smile and remembered how much the boys loved Lark. They were broken hearted over the breakup because of their closeness with her and that's why she couldn't deny Lark's access to them. It wouldn't have been fair to the boys. Fortunately, her brother kept her whereabouts a secret as he was asked to do so.

"Hey, little sister." Shayan greeted with a smile and hugged her.

"It's good to see you Shay." Rayne answered relieved and sought solace within her brother's loving hugged, which she needed. Shayan felt her tension and held her tightly, feeling her relax.

"It just got better bro." Rayne warmly answered, reluctantly releasing her hug and smiled lovingly at her brother.

Shayan wasn't pleased with what Lark had done to his sister, but his wife Holly and him loved her like a sister so, it made it very difficult to push her out of their lives. The three made a deal that they would not discuss Rayne when Lark would visit them, which suited everyone.

"What brings you by here?" Rayne asked happy, yet confused and glanced over at the boys who sat on Lark's lap inundating her with question after question which she sat patiently answering each one. She loved the boys and didn't mind the questions at all.

"Well, Lark called and asked us to stop by and see you. She explained everything that was going on." Shayan explained as the pair took a seat.

"Where's Holly?" Rayne asked with concern as to the where her sister-in-law was.

"She wasn't feeling too well today so, she decided to stay in the condo to rest."

"Is everything alright with the baby? Should we send someone over to be with her?" Rayne worriedly asked about Holly who was almost eight months pregnant now.

"Easy Rayne she's fine. Her mother is there with her." Shayan answered reassuringly to get his sister to calm down.

"Okay, I can't help that I'm protective of my niece and Holly." Rayne answered with a laugh and relief that Holly and the baby were fine. "Are you all out here on vacation or business?" Rayne asked and turned away when Danielle entered the room.

"Hey Rayne! Did I hear there's a party in here?" She asked teasingly and smiled.

"Good morning Danielle this is my brother Shayan and my two nephews, Brandon and Cole." Rayne proudly replied as she conducted the introductions, knowing the boys paid no attention to them.

"Nice to meet you Shayan." Danielle greeted with a smile as she shook his hand.

"Same here." Shayan answered with a cordial smile.

Lark looked up to see Danielle having an animated conversation with Rayne and Shayan, which made her jealous. Hell, Danielle made her jealous from the moment she first saw her. The woman was beautiful with long blond curls, hazel eyes and well-toned body to die for, Lark noted as she watched the attractive blond who stood entirely too close to Rayne, which pissed her off.

'I don't know for sure if Danielle and Rayne are dating or just friends, but from Danielle's body language you would think they were more than just friends.' She inwardly fumed, her jealousy mounting. Lark felt like she was moving in on her territory, her family and she had no right too. *'But then again what right do I have to think and feel that way considering what I did to Rayne?'* She realized and returned her focus back to the boys.

"Well, I'm going to grab something to eat before all the other grubs get in there and take it all." Danielle replied with a laugh and headed into the other room.

Lark's employees knew they were always welcome in her room at anytime, which put forth a relaxed atmosphere. She constantly had her handlers around at all times which worked out perfectly for Danielle's cover by joining the crowd in search of any pertinent information that might reveal the culprit. Lark's agent and accountant where both out of town on business which cut down on the craziness of the room.

Shayan lifted an eyebrow and smiled at Rayne as Danielle passed him. Rayne's blues met his and she laughed, shaking her head no to let her brother know they were only friends. "Just checking." He confirmed with a cocky smile much the same as the one Rayne possessed. "Hey, Lark." Shayan replied and walked to the couch.

"Hey, Shay. It's great to see you." Lark greeted with a smile and leaned up to receive the kiss Shayan was offering her. As many times as Lark saw the two of them together, she found it hard to believe they weren't twins. In fact, there was two years in age difference between the both of them, but they looked like identical twins. The same could be said for Rayne's younger brother Jayce and if you put the three of them together they could be triplets. Lark always found Rayne to be the best looking of the three of them, obviously.

Lark remembered how Rayne and her had discussed having children and how she wanted the child to possess Rayne's striking features, in particular those incredibly sexy blue eyes much to Rayne's protest who wanted the children to have Lark's green eyes, but Lark won out. So, they considered asking one of her brother's to be the sperm donor for when Lark was ready to conceive a child. Her heart raced every time she thought about having children with Rayne. She wanted that more than ever as she watched Rayne playing with Brandon by holding him upside down, both laughing hysterically. Lark knew Rayne's sexy smile was still there, it was just buried and she knew calling Shayan to come over would make Rayne happy. She watched Rayne's interaction with the boys and knew she would be a great mother. Lark wanted to give birth to the children for them because she loved Rayne so much and wanted to give her a child. She realized that dream of her and Rayne having children together was just that, a dream. She screwed up that dream, her life and Rayne's life by what she had done and wondered sadly if she would ever forgive herself for the hell she put Rayne through.

'No.' I will never forgive myself.' She tersely reasoned as Cole kissed her cheek and hugged her, snapped her out of her thoughts. She smiled lovingly and looked down at him. "Thanks sweetheart. What was that for?" She asked, hugging him tightly.

"I forgot to thank you for taking us to see Star Wars so, I wanted to make sure that I did." He explained with a childlike wonderment about him.

"You did thank me, but I don't mind your hugs and kisses at all." Lark answered adoringly, kissing and hugging him tighter.

Lark was glad that the kids were in town for an extended stay when the movie opened, as she knew how excited they were to see Star Wars. Lark invited them as her dates to the premiere of the movie, which they absolutely loved and had a fabulous time seeing all of the characters from the movie at the after party. The three had their picture appear in a popular entertainment magazine, which they got a big kick out of, Holly told Lark the last time they spoke to one another.

Lark had only one wish and it was that Rayne could have been with them. She thought about how much she adored the children and loved having them in her life. It gave her a sense of family and she treasured every moment she had with them. She was an only child and Lark knew she would never be an Aunt so she made sure she savored every moment with the boys. Lark was ecstatic when Holly and Shayan asked her to be Cole's godmother. It meant the world to her and made her feel like she was a part of their family, and as if she had siblings of her own which she so desired. Her parents loved her dearly and gave her anything she desired except siblings. So, she grew up lonely and it was extremely important to her when Rayne's family made her feel like she was part of theirs.

"Hey, did you see Hazel yet? I know she had some yummy pastries." Lark asked Cole and smiled when his eyes widened with the mention of the pastries.

"I'm on it!" He answered with a laugh climbing off her lap and scrambling into the other room to join his father who had made his way in to find the tasty morsels also.

Lark watched adoringly as Brandon and Rayne lay on the floor talking. "Auntie Rayne, are we going fishing soon?" He asked and stretched out on his side facing Rayne, with his head propped up on his hand just like Rayne.

"Don't we always go on a big fishing trip every summer?" Rayne asked her godson with a smile.

"Yes, but I want to go soon. Will Auntie Lark be going with us?" He asked excitedly and both glanced over at Lark.

Lark smiled and her breath escaped when two sets of piercing blue eyes stared at her. "We'll see sweetheart." Lark answered non-committing and caught her breath unsure of what she should say.

Brandon looked at Rayne and they began to laugh. "She hates fishing because she doesn't like to get her hands smelly." Brandon teased, as they laughed harder.

"Hey, you better behave young man." Lark jokingly warned and crawled on the floor, to tickling him.

Rayne watched the pair and was amazed at how well they got along. "Lark, he's a wimp. Look, he's already turning blue." Rayne laughed as Lark stopped tickling him and helped him stand up to catch his breath.

"You okay?" She asked with concern as she checked him over and looked into his gorgeous blue eyes, the same feature she loved so much about Rayne.

"I'm fine babe." He conceitedly answered with Rayne and Lark unable to contain their laughter at his comment.

"I think you've been around your Auntie Rayne a little too much." Lark chuckled and gave Rayne a sideways glance.

"No, not enough. He would have been worse if he were around me more. That must be from daddy." Rayne suggested with a laugh and sat up next to Lark, who thoroughly enjoyed the closeness.

"Auntie Lark, why don't you live with Auntie Rayne? She loves you don't you know?"

Lark was taken back by his statement and wondered if Rayne had mentioned that she still loved her in front of the kids. Rayne looked down at the ground in disbelief at the child's honesty. *'Damn, it's not bad enough that Lark is desperately trying to rekindle our relationship and now my nephew is in on it.'* Rayne cursed silently and wondered how they were going to get out of that one. "Is that so Brandon?" Lark asked curiously and glanced at Rayne to see her reaction of disbelief then turned back to him.

"Uh-huh." He answered with a shake of his head yes. "Oh, Auntie Lark, I don't want you to go away again, I love you." Brandon sighed with sadness and hugged her tightly.

Rayne looked at Lark who had tears streaming down her face. "Hey, buddy. Auntie Lark will always be there for you." She answered reassuringly and tussled his dark hair as Lark wiped the tears from her eyes. "Why don't you go make sure your brother isn't eating all of the goodies?" Rayne suggested so Lark could quell her emotions away from him.

"Okay!" He exclaimed as he broke the hug and ran into the other room.

Rayne reached to put her hand on Lark's back to comfort her, but pulled back. Instead, she stood up and put her hand out to help Lark up who took the assistance provided gladly. Lark locked cloudy green eyes with blues. "I'm sorry I got so emotional it's just that his comment meant a lot, but it also hurt too." Lark answered with sadness as she wiped more tears away.

"Yeah well, you have to face the consequences for your actions Lark. It should hurt because I wasn't the only person you devastated." Rayne answered coldly and walked out, joining the others in the opposite room.

Lark fought to keep the tears that formed in her eyes from falling. *'Rayne doesn't have one kind word for me and it hurts down to the core of my being. I understood Rayne's feelings towards me and would probably be the same way if the tables were turned, but it is the hardest thing in my life to have to go through.'* Lark inwardly thought and walked into the bedroom unnoticed to dress for the day's activities.

Lark found it extremely difficult to watch the love of her life walk away from her not to mention seeing the pain, hurt and betrayal Rayne possessed in her blue eyes when she walked into the bedroom and saw her with another woman. It was definitely hard, but this was worse, knowing that the person you love dearly and who is standing before you, wants nothing to do with you except to be out of your life. Lark could no longer hold her tears back and let them fall. She felt sorry for herself and she knew she had no right too. Lark saw a spark of hope in Rayne's devastatingly gorgeous blue eyes and refused to give up hope no matter how bitingly harsh Rayne was to her.

Lark finished dressing and headed out to join the rest of the crowd trying to keep up a stoic facade despite her sadness.

"We should be going Lark." Rayne told her, hugging and kissing the boys, then her brother.

"Yes, we don't want to be late." Lark answered with a strained smile as she hugged and kissed the boys goodbye also.

"Shay, tell Holly I'm sorry I didn't get to see her and I hope she feels better." Rayne replied as everyone walked towards the door.

"I sure will. She'll appreciate your thoughts. Hang in there Ray and don't give up hope. There was a reason the Fates put you two back in each other's lives. So, take a long look at what you had before and don't be so quick to push that aside. Maybe you'll find that what you had before was so wonderful that it will allow you to forgive her for her indiscretions." Shayan sincerely suggested and hugged her again.

"I don't know about that bro. I think it's a dead issue." Rayne rebuffed and glanced over at Lark, then back to her brother. It was hard for her to look at Lark without seeing the image of her that night with the other woman. *'The thought of that woman touching Lark makes my skin crawl.'* She thought with a shiver at the thought.

"Give it a chance and really look into your heart for your true feelings. I really hate to see you so unhappy Goonie bird and whether you want to admit it or not, I can see in your eyes that you still love her." He informed with a smile as he patted her on the back.

"I'll consider it and you knock it off with the Goonie bird thing. You know I hated it when you called me that as a little kid." Rayne teasingly warned.

"That's why we continued to call you that just to piss you off!" He answered with a laugh and left the hotel suite with a little boy on each side of him holding his hands.

Rayne watched them leave and was stunned by what her brother had said to her. The hand that touched her arm startled her

43

and she quickly turned her head around to find Danielle standing next to her.

"Are you okay Rayne?" She asked concerned as she gazed into Rayne's confused blue eyes.

"Aah, yeah. I'm fine." Rayne answered nodding her head in agreement.

"Okay, you looked like something was bothering you. I'll meet you both out front in a couple of minutes." Danielle answered when she walked past Rayne out the door.

"Yeah, okay thanks." Rayne stammered, still shaken by what her brother had said to her. She walked back into the suite to grab her briefcase and wondered if he saw something she just didn't see in herself. Rayne looked at Lark who gathered her own belongings and had to admit she was an extremely beautiful woman who still excited her. She had a gorgeous smile that made her heart skip a beat and green eyes that made melted her heart when she looked into them, but Rayne just couldn't get past what she did to her and she felt nothing but hate for the woman.

"Lark, let's get going." Rayne sternly ordered blocking her previous thoughts out of her mind and replaced them with disdain. Lark sighed disappointingly and followed Rayne out the door.

They silently waited at the elevators for the door to open. As much as Rayne hated to have to do it she knew she needed to thank Lark for calling her family for a visit. She really needed it and their visit lifted her spirits. Rayne looked down at the ground. "Aah, thanks for calling my family over for a visit. It was a very nice gesture." Rayne gratefully commented and took in a deep breath feeling awkward. *'There, that's out of the way.'* She thought relieved as the elevator doors opened and they stepped on.

"I'm glad I could make you happy. I've missed your beautiful smile." Lark answered and looked at Rayne who hit the buttons on the elevator.

44

'Why does she have to go there? She acts as if I'm the one that just walked out of the relationship and she had nothing to do with the end of it. She is in some serious denial.' Rayne thought irritated with her reluctance to admit she was the one who was wrong and pulled her gun out, checking her ammunition supply. *'She was the fucking cause of it ending and she just doesn't get it!'* Rayne angrily thought, tucking her gun back in the holster and turned to Lark with fiery blue eyes. "Lark, you're the cause of my unhappiness. You weren't concerned with my happiness before so, why do it now?" She angrily snapped.

"Because I want to make it up to you and I feel terribly guilty." Lark answered through cloudy green eyes.

"You are unbelievable Lark!" Rayne told her furiously. "Do you really think you can make up for what you did by bringing my family over for a visit? You're incredible, and you should feel guilty for what you did to me!" Rayne added with fire in her eyes as the veins in her neck stuck out from her hot temper.

"You're right Rayne. I can't make up for it, but I would like to try too." Lark offered, hopeful that Rayne would allow her to as the elevator doors opened and they stepped out heading towards the lobby to the limo.

"Don't bother." Rayne shot back in response as they climbed into the limo.

"Rayne, please." Lark pleaded.

"Lark, don't talk to me. I don't want to hear anything from you." Rayne demanded, opening the window and handing Danielle the directions to the autograph session Lark was required to attend.

Lark sat and quietly reflected as she looked out the window. *'I've got to figure some way to break through that tough exterior and get her past all that hate.'* She thought trying to figure out a way to win Rayne back and felt Rayne shift back in the seat and glanced over to her.

"Don't do it Lark, not one word." Rayne firmly demanded as she looked at her paperwork-knowing Lark was about to talk to her. *'She's persistent and a pain in the ass. I have to giver her that much, but then again that's the reason I fell in love with her in the first place.'* Rayne thought, as she remembered how determined Lark was in her pursuit of a date with her. *'If she wasn't as persistent as she was, I would never have agreed to a date and then would not have fallen in love with her. But then again, she wouldn't have broken my heart like she did. What a catch 22 situation.'* Rayne thought and shook her head in disbelief as anger welled in the pit of her stomach at the thought of Lark's betrayal. She wished she could put it past her and move on. Actually she had done just that until she got this bogus assignment. *'What a cruel freaking joke this was.'* Rayne thought and rubbed her forehead to alleviate the pain from her wicked headache.

They reached their destination for Lark's autograph session, which lasted the remainder of the day. Lark was very accommodating to her fans and loved to personalize her autographs, which took her much longer than other stars that usually zipped through the lines.

Lark was finishing up the autograph line much to Rayne's delight who sat next to her and handed her the pictures the fans wanted autographed as a fan approached and excitedly asked Lark, "Would you mind if I took a picture with Rayne and then with the both of you?"

Lark smiled knowing Rayne was going to hate having her picture taken with the fan as it embarrassed her and Lark looked at Rayne who had an obvious look of displeasure from the expression on her face.

"I'm sure she would love to, but you don't need my permission. Ask her yourself." Lark suggested with a smile as she looked up at the fan and began to autograph the picture she handed her.

"May I Rayne?" She asked with a smile as Rayne strained out an embarrassed smile.

"Now that Lark gave her seal of approval I suppose I could do it." Rayne answered with disdain from the request, but tried to be pleasant and she didn't want to miss an opportunity to needle Lark with her comment.

"Oh, excellent!" She exclaimed sitting in Rayne's lap much to Rayne's surprise as her friend snapped a picture of them.

Lark laughed inwardly knowing Rayne hated the limelight that was directed towards her. She was content to hang in the shadows as Lark fulfilled her celebrity duties of pictures and autographs. Rayne had been unnerved when fans approached her for a picture and an autograph. She couldn't understand why someone would want that from her she told Lark who in turn told her that it was because she's gorgeous and there was no sense to not show the world her beauty.

Lark remembered telling her she could be a star and Rayne had been asked and offered many acting and modeling jobs by top agents. Lark tried to talk her into accepting the offers, but Rayne refused saying that wasn't her bag. She was content with the job she had with the Secret Service.

"Okay, now with you both." The fan requested as Lark leaned closer to fit in the picture with the girls' friend taking the picture. "Thank you so much." The fan answered excitedly as she stood up from Rayne's lap and moved along off stage.

Lark looked at Rayne who had an embarrassed look on her face and she began to laugh as she took the next picture to be autographed from Rayne. "What?" Rayne gruffly asked confused by what Lark was laughing at.

"You're embarrassed." Lark teasingly laughed and autographed the picture while fans took her picture.

"I am not." Rayne stammered trying to keep up her stoic image and to conceal her embarrassment.

"You are too!" Lark teasingly accused with a heartier laugh, "and you're blushing too!"

Rayne couldn't contain it any longer and began to laugh too. "I guess I am huh? That was a very strange request for me to take a picture." Rayne answered, chuckling.

"Not really people used to ask me if they could do that all the time. You're gorgeous and they know it. They can't help but want a picture with you and she was a lucky woman to get to sit in your lap." Lark answered with a laugh and a wiggle of her eyebrows.

"Yes, she was wasn't she?" Rayne answered cockily and realized she was actually having a civil conversation with Lark. She instantly put her wall back up as she wasn't about to let Lark to weasel her way back into her heart that easily. "Jealous?" Rayne snapped sarcastically and stood up after the last fan passed by her, walking over to Danielle to inform her that they would be leaving soon.

"Yes, I am." Lark whispered sadly out of earshot of Rayne and stood up to thank the people who arranged the autograph session. She took pictures with each of them and posed for pictures for fans that stayed later.

Danielle left to get the limo to meet them at the exit Rayne chose. Rayne walked over to get Lark moving to the next scheduled appearance at a movie premiere. "Lark, we're running behind. We need to get moving." Rayne advised as she interrupted her conversation.

"Okay." Lark answered, turning to Rayne then back. "I'm sorry I can't stay longer." Lark informed the staff with regret for having to leave so soon.

"Thank you so much for coming Miss Morgan." The appreciative woman replied with a sappy smile.

'Kiss asses.' Rayne thought and watched them fawn all over Lark. *'That's why I never wanted to get involved in the business. Way too many butt sniffers!'*

"Anytime." Lark answered with a smile that Rayne read as her butt sniffer smile, indicating Lark was thinking the same thing as her. They had made a joke of smile's one night and named certain one's and the one Lark just gave was the butt sniffer one for sure! Rayne chuckled as they walked away knowing that Lark could give a friendly smile, but inwardly was telling them they were a bunch of kiss asses which she hated. She wanted people to treat her like any other person.

"What?" Lark asked as they approached the door and wondered why Rayne was looking at her.

"I was just laughing at the butt sniffer smile you gave her." Rayne answered with a sly grin, giving Lark a sideways glance.

"Noticed that did you?" Lark asked with a laugh and blushed embarrassed hoping that no one else picked up on the look.

"It was very obvious." Rayne added with a chuckle and opened the door to the limo for Lark.

"Let's hope it wasn't to them." Lark added with a laugh and climbed into the limo.

The ride was quiet as Rayne studied the contingency plans as to what exits to use to get Lark in and out safely. She didn't like the idea that Lark had to enter in the front, but they wanted the stars to walk the red carpet for publicity purposes. Rayne checked periodically to make sure they weren't being followed. She grew more anxious as she thought about having to walk up the red carpet with Lark. It unnerved her to think about how they would be inundated by screaming fans and popping flashbulbs. She learned early on to wear sunglasses to cut down on the popping flashbulbs or else your eyesight was gone for a while. Her hands became clammy and she nervously and repeatedly wiped them off on her jeans as they drew closer to the theater.

Lark knew Rayne absolutely hated this and put her hand on hers to calm her. Rayne looked at Lark surprised and pulled her hand away quickly. "I'm sorry. You looked nervous and I thought it would help to calm you down it's just a habit I guess." Lark apologetically answered.

"Your touch used to do that Lark, but now it makes my skin crawl." Rayne answered, agitated as the limo stopped and she jumped out after Danielle opened the door to wait for Lark to step out. She wasn't going to allow Lark to give her affection privately, knowing that Lark was finding a way to slip back into her heart and she had to fight off the urge to take her back. *She has to admit to her role in this whole fiasco and apologize to me first. Then I'll see if I can forgive her.* Rayne inwardly reasoned and put her hand out to help her exit the limo and Lark looked up at her.

"Don't bother. I wouldn't want to make your skin crawl." Lark sarcastically and angrily told her when she exited the limo to a deafening roar from her fans.

"Touché." Rayne whispered with a sneer on her face as Lark passed and gave her a sideways glance to let her know she was not at all pleased with her. Lark walked close to the crowd to pose for pictures and Rayne moved in behind her placing her hand on her waist to guide her away from the crowd. "Not too close. You don't know who might be waiting." Rayne whispered in her ear with a fake smile for the cameras and guided her arm around Lark's waist. Lark smiled to hide her anger at Rayne as they walked into the building. They were escorted to their seats for the premiere in time for the start of the movie.

50

The movie finished and they headed into the premiere party with Lark holding Rayne's hand leading her to their table to be seated. Lark had decided that if Rayne was going to be a bitch with her so was she and made sure to take any advantage of holding her hand, knowing it would piss her off more.

"You really love this charade don't you?" Rayne asked, leaning close to Lark and whispering angrily into her ear, which drove Lark nuts. The closeness and her silky voice in her ear no matter how angry it sounded sent her fire blazing.

She was able to calm her racing heart and sarcastically asked, "I'm reveling in it. Wouldn't you if you were in my place?" growing more tired of Rayne's attitude.

"I would have thought you might have a little more consideration for my feelings seeing as how you're the cause of all my hate and unhappiness." Rayne snapped back in a whisper so others wouldn't hear her. "Oh, but stupid me to have thought that because had you been more considerate of my feelings before we would be happily married by now." Rayne angrily informed her and walked away from the table towards the bar. "Jack and coke! Make it a double!" Rayne tersely ordered agitated by what Lark had said to her. *'Chew on that one Lark.'* Rayne irritably thought, giving Lark a nasty look as she sipped the strong, tasty beverage enjoying every minute of her drink. The whiskey burned on it's way down, but it sure tasted good and calmed her nerves.

Lark sat solemnly and stunned as she thought about what Rayne had just said to her. *'Did Rayne really mean what she said about being married?'* She asked and thought back to their discussion about marriage, but had never finalized plans to actually do it. Lark wanted to be married to Rayne and wanted children with her, but she got the feeling that Rayne wasn't ready for the marriage commitment at that time and wondered if Rayne had just said that to hurt her.

'That's right Lark. I meant it.' Rayne silently though, answering Lark's question with a smirk on her face as if she knew

what Lark was thinking. The anger welled in the pit of her stomach along with the Jack Daniels that hit it like a firebomb and thought about how she had intended to ask Lark to marry her.

When they had their discussion on marriage she had been evasive because she intended to ask her on their anniversary. Rayne had already purchased the ring she wanted to give her long before their discussion took place and it took every bit of self-control she could muster to save the surprise until their anniversary.

That surprise was never to be revealed the night of their anniversary when Rayne found Lark in the arms of another, *'in our bed no less!'* Rayne thought horrified by the memory, which disgusted her. She didn't know why she kept the ring, but she still had it. *'Maybe I kept it to remind myself to never give my heart to another like that again.'* Rayne reasoned and drained the drink, setting the empty glass down on the bar.

"Ready for another?" The bartender asked as he picked up the empty glass.

"No, but thanks." Rayne answered and turned back around to an even worse nightmare, that was quickly approaching her! It was Sal a balding, flamboyant chubby, jovial agent who constantly hounded her to let him represent her. *'Damn!'* She silently cursed and looked for an escape, but she was cornered and had nowhere to run.

"Rayne! Daawling!" He drawled flamboyantly. " Don't you run from me you sexy thing!" He enthusiastically warned, while pointing at her with his moderately feminine voice.

"Hello, Sal." Rayne answered in an agitated growl as she was in no mood to deal with him right now.

"Ooh, you look so hot sugar! Please tell me you'll let me represent you for a modeling job?" He pleadingly asked, as he looked her over with delight. "If I didn't love men so much hmmm, I would have to fight Lark for you!" He exclaimed with a girlish giggle along with his feminine gestures of whipping a limp wrist around to make his point.

'Like I would have anything to do with this guy if I was interested in the male species, Tom Cruise Yes, Sal no way!' Rayne inwardly thought with disgust at the thought of it. "Sal, we go through this all the time. I'm not interested." Rayne refused his offer with mounting agitation along with a splitting headache. She considered downing the entire bottle of Jack Daniel's to put herself out of her misery.

"Come on it's for charity, please?" He whiningly asked and smiled hoping she would do it.

"What charity?" Rayne asked slightly defeated and not believing she was actually considering doing it, but how could she refuse for a charity?

"For HIV/AIDS research. A very prominent gay and lesbian magazine is donating proceeds from the next issue for the charity. We have other stars lined up for the magazine shoot as well and you would be a fabulous addition." He smiled with delight at the thought of her modeling for it and for him being able to represent her. Many people in the entertainment world had tried to land Rayne as a client, knowing she would make a killing modeling or acting and he wanted to be the one to do what everyone else couldn't, get Rayne Donovan as their client.

"What's in it for you?" Rayne asked skeptically and raised an eyebrow.

"Just to be able to represent you in this and any future assignments." He answered with a hopeful smile that she wouldn't back out of it.

Rayne thought about it and figured it wouldn't hurt to do it considering it was for a good cause. "Okay, I'll do it." She reluctantly answered much to Sal's delight.

"Aah fantastic!" He exclaimed joyfully and hugged her happily and repeatedly.

"Yeah, yeah. When do I have to do this thing?" Rayne asked embarrassed by his excitement.

"Tomorrow at noon." He answered with a sly grin and grimaced, thinking she would change her mind.

"Man, you work fast dude!" Rayne answered with shock at the time frame as he laughed and wrote down the address for where the photo shoot would take place.

"Lark, it's good to see you!" Ellen greeted excitedly and hugged her.

"Hey, Ellen. How are you?" Lark answered with a strained smile still hurting from Rayne's comments.

"I'm doing great! I'm really happy to hear that you and Rayne are back together. Where is she anyway?" Ellen asked and looked around the room but didn't see Rayne.

"Aah, cornered at the bar." Lark answered with a laugh and motioned with her hand where Rayne was located.

"Oh, geez Lark! How could you not get her away from that little scam artist?" Ellen asked with a laugh feeling sorry for Rayne.

"Aah, she can handle herself." Lark casually answered with a laugh, inwardly hoping she was miserable talking with the man.

"She is looking so good Lark!" Ellen observed with obvious enjoyment at what she saw as she watched her interact with Sal. "You are one lucky woman Lark. I don't know what I would do if I got to look into those sexy blue eyes everyday and to be held in those strong arms not to mention, having those sumptuous lips pressed against mine! I just don't know if my heart would allow that much excitement." She admitted, inwardly flustered as she thought about it as they stared at Rayne.

Lark's mouth watered, her heart raced and warmth swept across her body at Ellen's description of Rayne. She desperately wanted those strong arms wrapped around her and absolutely needed to feel those lips against her own to taste Rayne, to feel her love again. "Well, Ellen a woman's go to do what a woman's got to do and some of us are more fortunate than others. I'll catch you later." Lark answered with a laugh and quickly walked over to Rayne desperate to be near the tall, dark and gorgeous woman as her desire for her escalated.

Lark finally made it to the pair and could tell Rayne was growing more agitated with Sal. "Hey, Sal. I'm going to steal Rayne from you." Lark informed him with a smile and grabbed Rayne's hand, leading her onto the dance floor. Rayne's touch sent a rush of electricity straight to Lark's center and she inhaled deeply to calm her pounding heart.

"Okay, good to see you Lark and I'll see you tomorrow Rayne." He shouted as the pair briskly moved away from him.

Rayne was happy to get away from him, but she went from one frying pan into another. *'At least this one was better looking.'* She reasoned with a chuckle as they began to dance. The song changed to a sultry Latin song, "Bailamos" by Enrique Iglesias, a song that Rayne absolutely loved. "Great song." She commented as the rhythm consumed her and she drew Lark into her arms, beginning to dance a slow salsa dance with her.

Lark's breath escaped her when she met smoldering blue eyes and felt Rayne's body move sensually against her own. Her legs felt weak and she was lucky Rayne had a tight hold on her while they danced or she would have been in a heap on the floor. Her body temperature rose as Rayne stared into her green eyes and erotically guided both of their bodies through the sultry dance. *'Oh, she is so beautiful and exudes sex appeal. She captivates everyone when she steps into a room with her sexy confidence.'* Lark admiringly thought, her heart racing faster when Rayne spun her around and drew her back in close to her body as their eyes met in a stare once again. A lump formed in Lark's throat along with her arousal that escalated. *'Oh, please kiss me.'* She silently pleaded and hoped Rayne would plant those sumptuous lips on her own. *'This is driving me nuts!'* Lark thought and felt weak at the knees again as Rayne began to sing the chorus to the song.

Rayne caught the weak kneed woman and pulled her back up close to her and flashed a sexy, cocky smile knowing she was driving Lark nuts with the dance. *'She's beautiful. I can't deny that, but I can deny her trying to weasel herself back into my life as if nothing happened.'* Rayne thought as they continued with their sultry dance.

'I want her so bad I can taste her.' Lark thought, staring deep into her blue eyes and lost herself in them. "Kiss me Rayne." Lark whispered seductively and moved up to meet Rayne's lips that never met hers.

Rayne leaned her head back to avoid Lark's advances with bewilderment as to what Lark was doing. "Why would I do that Lark?" Rayne asked, scrunching up face and agitated by the absurdity of Lark's request.

Lark was snapped out of her trance and swallowed hard and blinked her eyes repeatedly to refocus her thoughts on something other than those blues eyes. She quickly glanced side to side and looked back up into those alluring blue eyes and replied, "Because people are watching us and I thought maybe you would want to?" Lark informed her and asked with a smile, hoping she would capture her lips and devour them with her own. Her mouth watered with desire and anticipation to be kissed by her stunning ex-lover.

Rayne laughed, "Are you whacked? I could care less who is watching us and I really don't want to kiss you Lark." Rayne told

56

her with obvious agitation and began to walk away, but Lark held her there.

"Why don't you want to kiss me Rayne? Are you afraid you might feel something other than hate for me?" Lark asked with hurt in her voice at the turn in the mood of Rayne.

"You ARE whacked woman!" Rayne answered with a laugh as she shook her head in disbelief. "By the way, I'm positive I wouldn't feel a thing." Rayne added arrogantly with a smug look on her face, looking down at the shorter woman.

"Let's see then." Lark answered in a whisper, leaning up and pressing her lips against Rayne's as a photographer snapped their picture. Lark was oblivious to the photographer as her heart raced and warmth swept over her from the kiss.

'Damn photographers! They're friggin everywhere!' Rayne thought agitated by the intrusion, breaking the kiss and looking down at Lark, waiting for her to open her eyes.

"Well?" Lark asked dreamily as she was still caught up in the sensuality of the kiss.

"Nothing." Rayne smugly answered with a look of annoyance and boredom.

"Let me try again." Lark suggested seductively and once again pressed her lips against Rayne's, slipping her tongue past her lips for a deep, soul-searing kiss. Lark broke the kiss and looked up at Rayne. "Now, tell me you didn't feel something wonderful." Lark replied assuredly that she felt the undeniable passion from their shared kiss.

"No, I felt disgusted actually." Rayne answered in a lie. She had never felt such a kiss filled with so much love and caring from Lark. It rocked her world like never before, but she was not about to go down that road again with Lark. She devastated her once already which was more than enough for one person in their lifetime and she couldn't put herself through that again, as much as she desired the woman.

"You're such an ass face!" Lark shouted at Rayne as her admission felt like an arrow straight through the heart. She began to cry and rushed off the crowded dance floor leaving a very embarrassed and regretful Rayne standing in her shadow.

'Damn it!' Rayne inwardly cursed, regretting what she said to Lark and headed through the crowded dance floor to find Lark with no luck.

Rayne made it off the dance floor and bumped into Sal again. "What did you say to Lark? She's very upset." He asked with concern and agitation with Rayne.

"Which way did she go?" Rayne urgently asked, discarding his question as she looked around for her to no avail.

"She went out the back door." He told her and pointed to the door.
"No!" Rayne responded angrily and concerned and immediately ran towards the door. She had tightness in her chest and a bad feeling in the pit of her stomach when she approached the door. 'What the hell is she thinking going outside without me?' Rayne inwardly questioned and burst through the door to find two men holding Lark, who desperately struggled to break free while they pulled her towards their car. "LARK!" Rayne anxiously and fearfully shouted.

III

Rayne's adrenaline pumped and her heart raced as she ran towards the trio who held Lark. She tackled one assailant at full speed knocking everyone to the ground. Rayne head butted him knocking him out cold and back flipped off the man to take care of the other assailant who still held Lark. Rayne swung her leg around and kicked him in the face when he attempted to stand, sending him back to the ground in a heap. Rayne rushed to Lark's side that lay on the ground crying hysterically. "Are you okay?" Rayne worriedly asked as she knelt beside her. "Come on. I'll help you up." Rayne softly offered, taking Lark's hand and felt her trembling uncontrollably.

"Rayne!" Lark fearfully cried and moved closer to her crying harder.

"Hey, it's okay baby I'm here." Rayne compassionately reassured her and gathered Lark into her arms to calm her down. Lark wrapped her arms around Rayne's neck tightly, burying her face in her neck as she continued to cry.

Rayne hated it when Lark cried. It broke her heart every time Lark did it. "Come on now. Calm down, I've got you. You're going to be okay." Rayne whispered reassuringly in her ear and stood up with Lark in her arms. Rayne reached into her pocket to grab her phone and struggled to hold Lark as she turned the phone on. She was finally able to turn the phone on and hit speed dial to contact Danielle. "Where in the fuck are you?" She angrily shouted into the phone. "We're at exit three where you're suppose to be! Get back here I've got two assailants out cold waiting to be cuffed!" She shouted demandingly when she heard where Danielle was and clicked the phone off. Rayne noticed one of the assailants waking up and walked over to reacquaint him with the bottom of her foot, assuring he would be fast asleep once again as the limo screeched to a halt in front of her.

"What the hell happened?" Danielle asked as she rushed out of the limo pulling her handcuffs out.

"She was attacked. What the hell were you doing?" Rayne asked agitated with her, watching Danielle handcuff the one assailant.

"I was at the exit that was on the paper I received at breakfast this morning." Danielle informed her.

"Well, it was the wrong one Danielle!" Rayne angrily shouted and walked over to the limo, to put a Lark in it that was slightly calmed down.

"No, please don't let me go I'm terrified Rayne." Lark pleaded, crying harder and clutched her tighter.

"Aah, okay just settle down it's going to be alright Lark. I promise." Rayne softly guaranteed trying to calm the hysterical actress down while she sat inside the limo with Lark still clinging tightly to her. Rayne called in back up to pick up the suspects as Danielle finished handcuffing them. Rayne comfortingly held Lark and lovingly stroked her arm, to calm her down. Within minutes back up arrived and escorted the men off for interrogation.

Lark had fallen asleep, much to Rayne's delight. The crying finally stopped as Lark kept her tight hold on Rayne. Rayne still cared for Lark; she knew that as she held her in her arms. *'As much as I hated what Lark did to me, I don't want to see her physically harmed.'* She thought as the limo pulled up to the entrance of the hotel. "Lark, hey." Rayne whispered to wake her, brushing Lark's long blond hair off her face and noticed her sleepy green eyes look up at her. "We're at the hotel." Rayne informed her as Lark moved off of Rayne's lap.

"I'm sorry Rayne." Lark answered nervously as she ran her fingers through her long hair and pulled it off her face.

"Its okay, come on." Rayne answered caringly, grasping Lark's hand and helping her out of the limo.

"Rayne, I'll brief you later. I'm heading off to the interrogation to find out what's going on." Danielle informed her after exiting the limo.

"Yeah, let me know what happens." Rayne answered with a slight smile as the pair headed up to the suite.

Rayne had instructed Lark's staff that everyone was to leave the hotel with them therefore, decreasing the risk of bugs being planted while they were gone. The hotel staff was informed that the suite would be cleaned when they were present and a detail would inconspicuously stand guard near the room when they were gone so, there was no need to do a sweep for bugs every time they entered the room.

Rayne unlocked the door and turned on the light seeing that Lark looked a mess from crying. "You okay?" She asked with concern.

"No, I'm not okay! I was nearly kidnapped tonight because of you!" She accusatorily shouted and glared at Rayne to get her point across.

"Because of me?" Rayne asked with anger and disbelief, pointing at herself. "You're blaming me for this?" Rayne asked with mounting agitation.

"Yes, you didn't need to say what you did Rayne and for being an ass!"

"Incredible Lark! You're to blame for everything that has happened between us!" Rayne heatedly shouted and moved closer to her. "I'm here to help you despite the fact that I hate being here and now you want to blame me for this? I don't think so!" Rayne retorted in a raised tone with fiery blue eyes.

"You hate being around me that much?" Lark angrily asked as tears filled her green eyes.

"More than you would ever want to know Lark!" Rayne furiously shouted and stopped Lark's hand that swung around to slap her face, and thwarted the same attempt of the other hand. "What do you want from me Lark?" Rayne asked in a raised tone, holding Lark's wrists and pulling her closer. Blues met with greens and the desire for one another was evident. Rayne was pissed at Lark, but she wanted nothing more than to take her right there and then. She was hot for her and this latest argument ignited her simmering fire for Lark for some strange reason. "Is this what you want?" Rayne asked, pressing her lips against Lark's and aggressively exploring her mouth with her tongue. "Or is this what you want?" She asked through the kiss, pushing her against the wall and deepening the kiss.

Lark's passion mounted and her heart pounded through her chest. It was exactly what she wanted, to have her alluring lover's lips and body pressed against her.

Rayne's excitement heightened as she continued the deep, moist kiss. It had been a long time since she had sex and that's just what she wanted, sex, *just sex,* she reminded, *nothing more.* Rayne let go of Lark's arms that were pinned above her head and ripped open the front of her blouse, finding two perky breasts with hardened nipples ripe for the taking. She groped both breasts roughly and sank her teeth into Lark's neck, sending a rush of desire straight to Lark's center.

Lark's gentle and caring lover was replaced by a rough, aggressive one, which scared her yet, excited her at the same time. *'Maybe it excites me because it's Rayne whose back in my arms again,'* she surmised, and wished her caring, attentive lover were back, but she wasn't going to complain now that Rayne was pressed against her.

Rayne ran her tongue down Lark's chest capturing an erect nipple in her mouth and began to suckle the perky nipple and pinched Lark's opposite nipple between her fingers, sending waves of pleasure throughout Lark. Lark's breathing increased, and she ran her fingers through Rayne's raven hair as Rayne moved to the other breast.

"That feels so good Rayne." Lark moaned attentively watching her attractive lover. She loved to look at Rayne's dark features and thought about how sexy Rayne's mouth looked wrapped around her breast. *'Not to mention how incredible it feels to have her there.'* She thought as her body burned with desire. Rayne slipped her hand up and under Lark's skirt moving it to her firm backside. As expected by Rayne, Lark wore a thong, which made it easier for her to slide her hand under the material in her quest to find a moist opening to insert her finger.

Rayne's tongue worked it's way back up Lark's neck stopping in her mouth for a deep, moist kiss, Rayne's finger found the slick opening and slipped inside as Lark gasped in delight at the penetration. Lark wrapped her legs around Rayne's waist who walked towards the bed, continuing her desire filled kiss. Rayne slid her finger in and out of Lark's moist opening, which wrapped snugly around her finger as she approached the bed. Lark sank her fingernails into Rayne's back encouraging her to penetrate her deeper. "Oh, Rayne. You make me feel so good." Lark moaned through her kiss. Rayne laid Lark back on the bed, never breaking the kiss and slid her finger out to position Lark where she wanted her. Once in position, Rayne slipped Lark's thong off along with her skirt, lightly nibbling on Lark's hardened nipple. Lark pulled Rayne's shirt up over her head until she removed it along with her sports bra and caste them aside.

Once Lark was naked Rayne pushed two fingers inside the tight, wet opening and she lay on top of Lark, straddling her thigh. Rayne kicked her shoes off as she moved her fingers almost out of Lark and slid them back deep inside of her. *'I am so turned on and want to devour her so bad.'* She thought as her passion and her own wetness increased.

"Ooh, Rayne!" Lark exclaimed joyfully. *'Rayne's aggressiveness is rough, but it feels oh, so good.'* Lark inwardly thought and knew she could deal with it as long as it was Rayne inside of her.

Rayne desire for former lover escalated and Lark was just what she needed to satisfy her months of pent up sexual frustration. She didn't want to take time to make love. *'I just want sex, I want satisfaction in a hurry.'* She inwardly reminded, and her heart raced faster at the thought of achieving her goal.

Rayne sat up and continued to finger Lark's sex as she unbuttoned her pants with one hand and then unzipped them with Lark's help. Lark pushed Rayne's pants down to her ankles and Rayne lay back down on Lark and wiggled out of her pants using her opposite leg to remove them. It was quite a feat, but she finally removed the pants.

Lark's hands roamed Rayne's muscular, sexy, sweaty body as she nibbled on her neck. She moved her hips faster to match Rayne's rhythm with her fingers in and out of Lark's slick opening. She was in heaven from what Rayne was doing to her, her arousal escalating with each movement and she felt Rayne spread her folds pressing her wet, hot, sex against her thigh.

"Oh, baby. You feel so good." Lark whispered in Rayne's ear when she felt Rayne's wetness on her thigh. Rayne sucked Lark's hard nipple and stroked her sex against Lark's leg. Lark heard Rayne's labored breathing and put her hands on Rayne's backside squeezing it, which excited Rayne even more.

'That feels so good.' Rayne thought, feeling Lark's thigh against her hard clit. The movement was satisfying her urge to release her sexual tension. She moved her mouth to Lark's neck and began to lightly bite her neck. Rayne took Lark's free hand and guided it down between her legs. "Touch me." She huskily whispered before biting down hard on her neck and driving her fingers deep inside of Lark, who gasped out loud from the shear pleasure of it. Lark moved her hips faster, feeling her climax drawing near.

Lark ran her fingers against Rayne's slick, hot and hard clit as she moved her hips in rhythm with Lark's ministrations. "Oh, Rayne. I can't hold it any longer. I'm going to come." Lark moaned cuing Rayne to thrust her fingers in and out faster with her thumb massaging Lark's swollen nub as the first wave of Lark's climax began.

Rayne's sex was on fire and her climax began. She pressed her sex against Lark's hand and stroked her hips faster to reach her orgasm. Rayne felt Lark's opening tightening and knew her release was near and sank her teeth into Lark's neck again, feeling her sweet nectar release. "Aah oh, Rayne! Baby! Yes, yes!" Lark yelled as one orgasm after another racked her body. "Oh, Rayne. I want to feel your orgasm." Lark moaned pleadingly and felt Rayne's hot, labored breath against her neck. She felt Rayne's muscles tighten when her orgasm released, sending another shuddering wave of orgasm throughout her own body.

"Aah oh, aah." Rayne gasped trying to catch her breath and removed Lark's hand from her sex, leaving her swollen nub throbbing against Lark's thigh. Rayne laid her head down on the pillow next to Lark's neck spent and tried to calm her labored breathing, slowly removing her fingers from Lark's opening.

"Oh, oh, Rayne." Lark moaned as another wave of her orgasm released and she tilted her head back in pleasure when Rayne pressed her hand against Lark's pulsating nub to calm its passion.

Lark wrapped her arms around Rayne tightly and kissed her shoulder as their breathing calmed to a steady rhythm. "Oh, Rayne. I love you so much." Lark declared and held her tighter, turning to look at Rayne who quickly closed her eyes, pretending like she was asleep. Lark reveled in the wonderful feeling of having her love wrapped tightly in her arms. She felt the beat of Rayne's heart against her own and she knew this is exactly where she belonged. She thought about how ecstatic she was that Rayne was back as a satisfied smile slipped across her face.

'Bite me! This is not what I wanted! I only wanted sex nothing more and certainly no declarations of love from her.' Rayne thought and felt Lark kiss her lips lightly as she continued her ruse of pretending like she was asleep. *'Not very smart there Rayne. You think you would learn. What in the hell are you going to do now?'* She tersely asked and lay still on top of Lark. *'Just play it off like it was a one night- stand. That's what you're going to do.'* She told herself. She regretted what she had just done, but damn it she couldn't contain her desire for Lark and gave into her urges. She peaked Rayne's arousal and her hormones took over making her lose all her self-control. *'I may have just made the biggest mistake of my life.'* Rayne thought regretfully, waiting for Lark to fall asleep so she could get up and get away from her. Rayne lay completely still and waited, knowing it wouldn't be long before Lark was sound asleep. She was right, it took about fifteen minutes before the woman was fast asleep.

Rayne rolled up on top of Lark and looked down at the peacefully sleeping blonde. She watched her momentarily and wondered if maybe deep down she still loved her. She did still love her she decided, but she just couldn't get past the fact that she slept with another woman. The thought disgusted her and it sickened her more to think she just kissed the same lips and body parts the other woman kissed. It nauseated and pissed her off to think about it. She got up out of the bed and rushed into the bathroom to get Lark's scent off of her.

Rayne took a long shower scrubbing her body and her teeth; to make sure Lark was completely off of her. *'Damn it! That was stupid Rayne.'* She inwardly admonished despite the fact that it felt great to have sex again and climbed out of the shower. She toweled off before dressing in a T-shirt and boxer shorts for bed. She went out and laid on the couch wide-awake, unable to fall asleep, thinking about how stupid she was. *'Just get your non-caring, sex only, no love involved attitude back. The one you had before you lost your heart to Lark and decided to love someone. Life was much easier then with a different woman every night, less attachments and heartache',* she thought and finally drifted off to sleep

Rayne slept for a few hours and woke up before Lark. She wished she could just get out of there and away from Lark. She didn't want to face her first thing this morning, as she knew Lark would take last night differently than what she had done. She was stuck there and decided to concentrate on her morning Martial Arts workout, hoping it would release some of her frustration. Rayne poured herself into her workout and cleared her mind of everything except the movements she went through.

Lark woke to the sunlight peaking through the blinds and she smiled as she was filled with joy and happiness. She stretched and rolled over to find Rayne was not in bed. She was disappointed, but not that much after last night's love making with Rayne. It was wonderful and she felt gloriously. *'There is no way this smile is coming off of my face.'* She thought happily. Lark was ecstatic that her lover was back and wished she would join her in bed for round two, as a mischievous smile crept across her face as to what she had in mind for their next round.

Lark rolled over and saw Rayne through the door going through her routine. She lovingly smiled and intently watched the tall, raven-haired beauty move with so much gracefulness. She reveled in how sexy her muscles looked when they flexed with each movement. Lark always loved to watch Rayne workout and knew she hated to be interrupted so, she decided to just lie there and enjoy watching her.

Rayne turned and faced Lark with closed her eyes and her hands posed in front of her. She knelt her head and inhaled deep breaths as Lark looked on with a loving smile. Lark noticed Rayne had a navel ring now, which she found to be incredibly erotic on Rayne's well-toned and tanned abdomen. Lark smiled and wished Rayne was in bed with her so she could place soft kisses on that taut abdomen. She previously tried to convince Rayne that a small silver hoop navel ring would look very hot on her, but Rayne would never give in, until now. She wondered what had made her change her mind about getting one.

Lark's trance was broken when she heard a knock at the door and saw that Rayne's peaceful demeanor turned to one of agitation from the intrusion.

Rayne answered the door to find Danielle waiting there. "Good morning." Danielle greeted with surprise at Rayne's outfit of her sports bra, boxer shorts and her hair pulled back in a ponytail. *'I don't mind the outfit at all.'* She appreciatively thought, finding it hard to concentrate on what she needed to tell Rayne.

Rayne wiped the sweat off of her body as she opened the door wider for Danielle to enter. "Hey, what happened with the interrogation?" Rayne asked as Danielle sat down on the couch.

"It's still going on. They're pretty stubborn and won't talk." Danielle advised her, looking tired from being up all night.

Rayne grabbed a bottle of water and looked back at Danielle. "Hey, do you want something?" She offered and pointed at the small refrigerator.

"Yeah, a coke please. Maybe it will wake me up." Danielle answered with a laugh as Rayne sat next to her and handed her the soda.

"No luck with the guys huh?" Rayne asked disappointed and sipped her water.

"No, maybe we should have you go in and rough them up." She suggested with a laugh and found it hard to keep her eyes off of Rayne's scantily clad body.

"What went wrong last night?" Rayne asked confused by the turn of events and miscommunication the previous night.

"I'm not sure. Here's the paper I got with the exits marked and which one would be the target exit for Lark to use." Danielle explained and handed her the paper.

Rayne looked it over and realized it wasn't the one she had written, it had been changed. "Damn, where did you get this from?" Rayne asked confused and peered up at her.

"It was sitting on the counter by the food when I grabbed breakfast yesterday and I thought it was the copy that you left for me." She explained and sipped her soda.

Rayne noted the scribbled handwriting on the paper was a sorry excuse for her precise handwriting. She thought back as to who was in the room that day and noted the people, Hazel, Kim, Danielle and her brother. She scratched him off the list and wanted to do the same for Danielle, but was hesitant to do that just yet. "Can I get a copy of your report you wrote up from last night?"

"Sure, I just finished it, but I must warn you it's not typed yet and my handwriting is hideous." Danielle laughed with a shrug of her shoulders.

"No problem. I'll just make a copy of it and add some things that I can remember about the incident before you type it up." Rayne coyly explained to her.

Danielle pulled out the report from her folder and handed it to Rayne to make a copy, which Rayne scanned through the fax machine. "I'm heading off to bed to get some sleep. What time do you need me?"

"I'll give you a call when we need to head out. Sleep well." Rayne informed her and walked to the door with her as Hazel and Kim approached the suite to begin their daily routine.

"Good morning." Rayne greeted the two women who entered the suite.

"Good morning." They answered in unison as they headed into the suite to get started.

Rayne grabbed her cell phone and went out onto the balcony for some privacy with her phone call to her director. Rayne informed him of the events that took place the previous night and of her suspicions as to the people she considered to be the insider in the kidnapping conspiracy. She told him she had ruled Lark's accountant and her agent out from the beginning, but was suspicious of Kim, Hazel and unfortunately, Danielle. She didn't want to have to believe that Danielle was involved, but after the incident last night she couldn't effectively rule her out. She informed the director that she would fax a copy of Danielle's report along with a copy of the changed itinerary for a handwriting analysis to rule her out.

Rayne knew Danielle would know a handwriting analysis would be done and wouldn't be foolish enough to change the itinerary in her own handwriting. *'But, on the other hand, she may think that I wouldn't check her because we have worked together before and she knows I trust her.'* She inwardly surmised and decided it was safer to have her checked just in case. Rayne also informed him she would send a sample of handwriting from the other two suspects to be analyzed as well. Director Bailey assured her he would take care of everything and get back to her as soon as possible. Rayne clicked her phone off and entered the spacious suite once again to a lot of cheerful voices.

Rayne rolled her eyes and sighed as she walked towards the other room wishing it were quiet again. She grabbed a pear and sank her teeth into the tasty fruit as Hazel prepared the coffee. "Hazel, I need a list of supplies that you might need so, I can have them delivered okay?"

"Sure, I'll make one out in a few minutes." She answered and put the coffee grounds into the machine, looking back at Rayne with a smile.

"Great, thanks." Rayne smiled and took a few more bites of the pear and watched as Lark went through her exercises. She noted that Lark's body was more tone and that her work with the personal trainer had paid off. She was surprised Lark was so serious about her workouts because she never wanted to do it before.

Lark looked up and saw Rayne watching her and smiled happily, flashing her a wink as she moved into position for her next exercise. Rayne rolled her eyes and shook her head, quickly heading towards the shower.

'Great! She acts as if everything is back to normal.' Rayne thought tensely and climbed in the tub to take a shower. Rayne couldn't understand why Lark acted as if nothing happened and as if what she did wasn't wrong. Lark didn't even acknowledge that what she had done was wrong and it was as if she blamed Rayne for her turning to another woman. *'Why?'* She wondered and decided to stop thinking about it, as it only angered her more.

Rayne finished her shower and dressed in a black T-shirt and Khaki shorts before exiting the bathroom. She opened the door to find Lark standing before her naked. She was stunned and averted her blue eyes away from the attractive blonde.

"Why did you lock the door? I was going to join you." Lark seductively asked, moving closer to Rayne who side stepped her advance of a kiss and walked past her.

"I locked the door because I didn't want company." She answered gruffly and exited the room, leaving Lark standing in total disbelief from Rayne's bad mood.

'What in the hell was up with that?' Lark angrily wondered, closing the door to the bathroom and was overwhelmed by the familiar scent of Rayne's lotion and cologne. Rayne was a creature of habit and wore the scented "juniper breeze" lotion, always, along with her perfume "Curve." After Rayne left her, she had purchased the woman's favorite lotion and perfume to remind herself of Rayne. She knew it was silly to do, but she felt it gave her a connection to Rayne and besides, it put a smile on her face.

71

She inhaled deeply and climbed into the shower absorbing the fresh aroma.

Rayne sat at the desk and flipped on her laptop computer to get some work done. She wanted to do her own handwriting analysis to make sure no one, including Director Bailey, was involved in the conspiracy at headquarters. She entered the handwriting samples of Hazel, Danielle and Kim's. Lark provided Rayne with a copy of Kim's exercise program she had written out for her previously when Rayne was gathering information on her. Rayne plugged in all of the information and would have to wait for the computer to do the rest of the work. She had a buddy in the age~cy, which provided her the handwriting analysis program and was grateful he gave it to her. Her submitting the handwriting analysis to her boss was a formality and protocol for the case to be included in the file.

"Aah, Rayne." Kim stammered when she entered the room reluctant to speak with Rayne. She didn't trust Rayne for some reason and didn't like the uncomfortable feeling she got when the two of them were near one another. She didn't know why she felt that way, but she did.

"Yes." Rayne answered as her blue eyes peered up from the computer and looked at the personal trainer.

"I have an appointment with a potential client tomorrow and I wanted to make sure we wouldn't be leaving before then."

"No, we will be here tomorrow so, you won't need to worry about missing you're other appointment." Rayne answered cordially and looked back down at her computer.

"Okay, thanks. I'll see you tomorrow then." Kim answered and headed out the door.

"Yep, bye." Rayne replied without looking up and wondered why in the hell her computer was taking so long. She looked at her watch and realized they were behind schedule for the photo shoot.

"Shit! Lark! We have to go!" Rayne shouted out and stood up from the computer. *'I'll have to leave this running until I get back.'* Rayne thought reluctant to leave the computer running, but she had no choice if she wanted the program to finish.

Lark and Hazel entered the room as Rayne hurriedly gathered her things. "How did we get so far behind?" Lark asked with bewilderment.

"I totally forgot about the photo shoot." Rayne informed her, heading to the door and held it open for the women as they passed through.

Hazel headed back to her room as Rayne and Lark made their way onto the elevator. Lark made a move closer to Rayne as she wanted to kiss her attractive lover as she hadn't had a chance yet, but Rayne squatted down and opened her briefcase. She pretended to be looking for something to avoid the contact she knew Lark wanted from her. Lark stood twiddling her thumbs and watched Rayne wondering why she was being so evasive this morning.

"I'm glad you agreed to do this photo shoot Rayne. I didn't think you would agree to it when you knew I would be in it too."

The anger filled Rayne as she took in what Lark had just said to her. "What?" She snapped angrily, her eyes ablaze. "He didn't tell me you would be in it or that you were even involved with the shoot." She shouted agitated with the ruse and knew Lark had to be involved in it. "You knew about this all along and you put him up to it didn't you?" Rayne accusatorily asked, closing her briefcase and stood up with fiery blue eyes.

"Yes, Rayne I knew about it, but I told Sal to ask you. I didn't want to answer for you." Lark explained, surprised by Rayne's viciousness. "He didn't tell you we would be doing it together?"

"No, but I'm sure you knew he wouldn't anyway." Rayne answered with angered sarcasm and exited the elevator when the doors opened.

Rayne stormed over to the counter to pick up the rental car keys with Lark in hot pursuit. "Rayne, you have to believe me that I didn't tell him to hide it from you." Lark pleaded with her.

"Whatever Lark!" Rayne snapped as she turned and walked toward the lobby doors towards the exit and waited for Lark to catch up to her.

"I'm sorry for the misunderstanding Rayne." Lark replied regretfully.

"There's always a lot of misunderstandings with you isn't there Lark?" Rayne sarcastically asked, holding the car door open for her. Once Lark was in the car Rayne slammed the door behind her and walked to the driver side to take control of the car.

"Rayne." Lark whined and Rayne put her hand up to stop her conversation.

"I don't want to hear it Lark." Rayne warned, stomping the gas and speeding out of the parking lot.

Rayne checked the mirrors frequently and took unnecessary turns to ensure they weren't being followed, which she saw no evidence of, while Lark sat quietly looking out the window wondering how Rayne could change so much from last night when they made love. Maybe she read too far into it, but she couldn't believe that considering she felt so much love from Rayne when she they had sex last night.

Lark's cell phone rang and she clicked the phone on. "Hello? Hi daddy!" She excitedly greeted. "Yes, I'm okay and yes, Rayne is taking care of me. Well, sort of." Lark answered and glanced over to see if Rayne heard what she had said, which she found Rayne to be lost in her thoughts.

Rayne cussed herself for being so weak and having sex with Lark the previous night, oblivious to Lark's phone conversation. It was stupid of her and now she sent the wrong message to Lark that all was forgiven, which was far from the truth. *'That was a pretty dumb mistake you made Rayne. You know better.'* She inwardly admonished and steered the car in the parking lot of the small photography studio.

"Here, daddy wants to talk to you." Lark told her and handed the phone to Rayne who reluctantly took it from her.

"Hello." Rayne greeted enthusiastically when she put the phone to her ear to talk to the Congressman.

"How's my other favorite daughter?" He asked with a chuckle.

"Could be better sir." Rayne answered reluctantly.

"Is my daughter giving you hell?" He asked with concern.

"Yes, sir and I don't know how much more I can take of it to be honest." Rayne admitted, knowing she could talk to him honestly, despite the conversation being about his daughter.

"I understand how hard it is for you Rayne and I'm sorry my daughter has hurt you. I didn't want to take any chances with her life and I wanted you to be the one to protect her. I'm sorry that this is so hard for you."

"I can't imagine how you would know that sir." Rayne answered irritably and wondered incredulously, *'how the hell does he know how hard it is for me?'*

"Rayne, I know, believe me. Lark's mother cheated on me and I had the same feelings as you do." He explained as Rayne was shocked at the revelation and glanced over at Lark who was staring out the window. She was glad she didn't look at her because she would have seen a look of total disbelief and her eyes would have told her exactly what her father just did.

75

'I guess like mother, like daughter on that one.' Rayne thought still in shock from the fact that Lark's mother cheated on her husband.

"All I can tell you is that I'm glad that I decided to forgive her because my life is nothing without her. I hope maybe you can do the same because I truly believe that you two are meant to be together forever."

"I'm not too sure about that sir." Rayne answered evasively.

"Give it a chance hun. Listen, please don't say anything to Lark about her mother and I, she doesn't know."

"No, problem sir. We'll talk to you later." Rayne answered, happy that the conversation was coming to an end.

"Yes, and thank you very much Rayne." He answered and clicked the phone off followed by Rayne who still had a dumbfounded look on her face and opened the car door.

"Everything okay with daddy?" Lark asked with concern from the look on Rayne's face.

"Aah yeah, he just wanted to check on his little girl." Rayne answered with a slight smile as Lark did the same at the thoughtfulness of her father.

Rayne stepped out of the car and opened the door for Lark. "Rayne, why didn't we take the limo?"

"I have my reasons." Rayne answered coldly as the pair walked towards the door and Rayne held it open for Lark, who passed with a frustrated sigh from Rayne's evasiveness, as Rayne scanned the neighborhood for anything unusual.

"Lark, Darling!" Sal exclaimed happily as he approached and kissed her.

"Sal, you should have told her everything! She's pissed." Lark told him, aggravated by what he had done.

"I totally forgot hun." He answered with a chuckle and moved to greet Rayne. "I know you're mad at me sweets, but it was an honest mistake on my part. I'm sorry, please forgive me?" He pleaded with Rayne and gave her a puppy dog look.

"Just don't let it happen again little man." Rayne sarcastically warned and pointed at him to make her point, as she passed by him to get the photo shoot over with. "Okay, let's get moving." Rayne instructed the photographer. "I'm eager to get this finished."

"Why don't you go ahead and get changed. Lark is already in that room changing." He suggested and pointed to the dressing rooms. "Everything you need is in the room next to hers."

"Okay." Rayne answered and entered the dressing room only to find a towel. *'What the hell!'* Rayne thought agitated and exited the room at the same time Lark did and looked at the photographer.

"Where are the clothes?" Lark asked, slightly aggravated and looked at Rayne who gave her a disgusted look. "No way! I had nothing to do with this Rayne." Lark informed her adamantly and held her hands up in protest to the impending argument.

"Ladies, you will be covered in the front. I promise." Ian informed the two to reassure them.

"This is really fucking pissing me off and if it wasn't for a great cause I would be out of here!" Rayne announced loudly, entering the room and slamming the door. *'Why didn't I just walk out that door when I had the chance so I didn't have this freaking assignment? It's not like you need to work Rayne. You have plenty of money to retire now and just chill. You could be sitting at a Red Sox baseball game right now instead of this freaking torture.'* Rayne inwardly fumed, stripping down to her birthday suit and threw her clothes on the chair in disgust and wrapped the towel around her muscular body. She walked out with her hands on her hips and a scowl on her face to let Sal and Ian know she wasn't pleased. "Come on Lark what's taking so long?" Rayne asked impatiently.

"I'm not very fast at taking my clothes off unless you're standing in front of me." Lark shouted back with a snicker to lighten the mood, which she hoped it did and wouldn't piss Rayne off more.

Rayne chuckled and crossed her arms over her chest, shaking her head in disbelief. *I know this is a nightmare and just isn't happening to me. I wish I would wake up if it is a damn dream.'* Rayne thought, with a chuckle at the irony of everything, as Lark walked out of the dressing room with a mischievous smile. "You just love this don't you?" Rayne whispered as Lark passed by her.

"Beyond belief." She sarcastically answered, looking back over her shoulder with a sly grin and a wink.

Rayne rolled her eyes and sighed deeply, trying to fight of the desire to wrap her hands around Lark's throat and followed her to the set, impatiently waiting for her instructions.

"Okay Lark. I need to get a few of you alone and then I'll have Rayne join you." Ian instructed them as Lark approached the set to begin her photo shoot. Rayne moved to the window and checked the area again for anything out of the usual activities. She had a really bad feeling about this trip and wasn't sure why, but she didn't like it. She noted a black van at the corner in front of the bank and watched to see if anyone exited or entered the van. No one did after a few minutes, which she surmised, was unoccupied. Rayne thought maybe she was just being overly protective due to the bad feeling she was having today.

"Rayne! Rayne, I need you now." Ian hollered to get her attention and watched as the tall blue-eyed beauty casually strolled over.

"I need you to lay on your stomach right here please." He instructed her as she waited for Lark to cover herself and move over so Rayne could take her position.

Lark saw that something was bothering Rayne by the concerned look on her face as Rayne lay on her stomach where Ian instructed her too. "Now, Rayne I want you to rest your head on your arms which need to be crossed in front of you okay?"

"Sure." Rayne answered absently and was lost in her thoughts to which person was involved in this whole fiasco and did as Ian asked her too.

Rayne felt Lark slip her leg between her own legs and press her naked body against her back. Rayne turned her head over her shoulder and gave a sideways glance to look at Lark. "Are you okay?" She asked softly with concern.

"Not really. Did you tell Kim about this photo shoot?" Rayne curiously asked trying to piece everything together.

"Hmmm," Lark stammered, trying to remember if she did or not and went back through her conversation with the woman. "Aah no I didn't why?" She asked inquisitively.

"I was just curious." Rayne evasively answered and laid her head to the side resting it on her arms.

"Okay Lark. Bring your left hand to the side of Rayne in front of her breast and then lay your head against her back." Ian told her.

Lark slid her hand along the bed and brushed it against Rayne's breast. Rayne arched an eyebrow and looked back at Lark. "Sorry." Lark whispered sheepishly and moved her hand in position with Rayne laying her head back down.

Lark laid her head against Rayne's back and Ian positioned Lark's long blonde hair so it was draped across her back. "Almost ready ladies." He announced and readied his camera.

Rayne felt Lark's racing heart beat against her back along with Lark's curls against her firm backside. *'This feels so good.'* She thought, as her heart began to beat faster, and her body temperature rose from her arousal. *'Oh, how she wanted to take Lark's hand and place it between her legs to satisfy the throbbing sensation down there. Knock it off Rayne. You don't want to go there again. Get those thoughts out of your head!'* She demanded inhaling a deep breath and exhaling slowly to calm her arousal.

"Nervous?" Lark asked softly.

"You have no idea. I don't know how you do this kind of stuff on a regular basis." Rayne admitted with a chuckle and a better understanding of Lark's line of work.

"You'll get used to it." Lark answered with a laugh.

"That's just it Lark. I don't want to get used to it." Rayne answered coldly and glanced back at her, then moved back into position.

"Okay, here we go. Give me a couple of really sexy looks." Ian instructed them.

'Oh, bite me with the sexy looks crap!' Rayne thought agitated by the whole thing and could kick her own ass for agreeing to it as Ian began to take their picture.

"Okay now, give me an alluring, mischievous smile. Oh, yes fabulous." He enthusiastically replied as Rayne and Lark obliged. "Rayne, you are such a natural at this you should consider a career in this field.

"No, thanks. I'm happy with what I'm doing now." Rayne answered with a chuckle.

'I am so hot for Rayne. This is driving me nuts to lay here naked with the woman that I love and not be able to touch her.' Lark thought as her desire and need for Rayne peaked.

'He's a lucky guy to get to photograph naked women all day. Maybe I should take up photography.' Rayne thought with a laugh. *'Geez, how many pictures can he need in one position?'* She wondered and grew more agitated staying in this position, she just didn't want that closeness with Lark.

'I hope that Rayne can't feel how wet I am right now.' Lark thought slightly embarrassed. *'Well, maybe it wouldn't be so bad.'* She thought mischievously.

"Okay now, Lark. I want you to lay on your side with Rayne on her side behind you." Ian instructed her.

They moved into a 'spooning' position with Rayne behind Lark and her head resting in her hand with the sheet draped across Lark's sex. "Now, Rayne take your hand and place it on Lark's breast to cover it for the picture.

Rayne's touch sent a rush of warmth throughout Lark's body and she was positive she had an orgasm at that moment. Rayne's touch was so gentle and caring that Lark could hardly contain herself.

"Ladies, come on. You look so, aah mechanical. You're in love, show the camera that." He enthusiastically encouraged them.

"If he only knew what was going on he'd be really embarrassed by that statement." Rayne whispered in Lark's ear with a chuckle.

Lark didn't think it was funny. In fact, she was offended by it, but didn't say anything. It was terribly hard for her to be in the arms of the woman she loves with all her heart, and for that person to not reciprocate it. She was confused as to the message that Rayne sunt last night and she was saddened by it.

Ian finished his pictures for that pose and had Rayne lay on her back with Lark on top of her. Lark's arms were crossed over Rayne's chest and her chin rested on her arms as she gazed into Rayne's deep blue eyes. Lark stared into her eyes and wondered what Rayne was thinking. She wondered if she was thinking the same thing that she wanted, to slide down south and devour her sex! She knew she hurt Rayne to the deepest core of her being, but hoped she would forgive her and thought she had done just that last night. Lark knew there was still an undeniable attraction that Rayne had for her, she could see it in her eyes.

Rayne wondered as she stared into Lark's beautiful emerald green eyes how someone who had professed their undying love to her could sleep with another woman. No matter how many times she asked herself that question she couldn't come up with an answer. It only pissed her off more, as usual, which is exactly what it was doing right then. *'I have really got to stop dwelling on this crap and cut this Sybil act of, I love ya, I hate ya bit completely out.'*

"Okay, I've got all the shots I need of the two of you together. Now, I need shots of Rayne." Ian informed the pair and reloaded his camera.

Lark couldn't stand it anymore. She had to feel Rayne's lips pressed against her own as she was driving her absolutely crazy. Lark moved in for a kiss and sought entry with her tongue, which was denied by an unsuspecting raven-haired woman. She looked at Rayne with bewilderment as Rayne slipped out from below her to sit up. "Don't do that again Lark." Rayne coldly demanded, looking over her shoulder at her with disdain.

Lark wrapped the towel around her, slightly embarrassed by the unreciprocated advances and headed to the dressing room to redress with tears welling in her eyes from the rejection. *'I just keep setting myself up with her for failure. I can't take it any longer and I intend to have this mess hashed out once and for all.'* Lark thought, wanting to clear the air with Rayne.

'She just doesn't get it that she was wrong and that I shouldn't want anything to do with her. Well, she might have if you would have stayed out of her pants you idiot!' Rayne angrily thought and finished her individual pictures. She still loved Lark and wanted to be with her, but she couldn't. She knew it would never work for the reason that she wouldn't be able to trust her again. *'It's better for both of us this way and it will be less painful.'* Rayne reasoned sadly. She knew she had to do something so Lark would get it through her head that their relationship is finished. Rayne figured it might take some very hurtful words from her to get the point across that their relationship was dead. Rayne hated the thought of what she was going to have do by being nasty, but it had to be done. Rayne looked outside the studio and noticed the van was gone which put her more at ease. She headed into the dressing room and put her sports bra on as Lark walked in the room already dressed. "Do you mind?" Rayne asked, aggravated by the intrusion.

"You didn't mind it last night." Lark snapped back sarcastically.

"That was a mistake." Rayne angrily retorted at Lark's attitude and turned to face Lark defiantly.

"We need to talk Rayne." Lark angrily told her and placed her hands on her hips boldly.

"Not now. Not here." Rayne told her in an angry tone.

"No, now you are being very unfair..." Lark replied and tried to finish, but was interrupted by Rayne.

"What?" Rayne shouted without care as to who heard the conversation. She had enough of Lark's refusal to accept her consequences and with her attempts to win her back without acknowledging her indiscretions. "Fair?" Rayne asked, moving closer to Lark with only her bra on for clothing. "You want fair? Try this on for size Miss thing! How fair was it for me to find the woman that I loved more than life itself in bed with another woman on our anniversary? How fair was that? How fair was it for me to have to deal with that on top of the fact that my partner and grandmother who was very close to me died in the same week?" Rayne furiously shouted with fiery blue eyes and leaned closer to Lark, who was unable to control her anger anymore, with her emotions consuming her.

Lark began to cry as Rayne shouted at her and didn't know what to say in response. What could she say? "Stop crying and tell me damn it! You wanted to talk so talk! Tell me how it was fair for me to fly half way across the country with no sleep to come back from an assignment on our anniversary to surprise you and ask you to be my partner for life? Tell me, I'd really like to know." Rayne shouted louder with Lark crying harder as her guilt overwhelmed her and she was speechless. She felt horrible for what she had done to Rayne and with Rayne pointing everything out, it hit her worse. She was stunned. "Lark, it's over. We're finished." Rayne heatedly informed her and moved her hands horizontally in front of her to emphasize her point.

"I aah. I don't understand? What was last night?" Lark asked confused through her tears, looking up at Rayne.

Rayne laughed that she still just didn't get it and there was nothing else she could do to get the point across. "You were just a good fuck last night Lark!" Rayne shouted with a sarcastic grin on her face. She knew that would hurt Lark and hopefully end everything between them even though it hurt her deeply to do it. She felt awful about what she said to Lark especially when she saw that her comments devastated her when she looked into her green eyes. *'Payback is a bitch and I could kick myself for feeling bad about what I said to her after all, she's to blame for everything.'* Rayne thought to ease her guilt.

"You don't mean that Rayne." Lark tearfully answered, shaking her head in disbelief.

'She is so hard headed!' Rayne thought as her frustration with Lark mounted. "It hurts to know you were just a good fuck and to be tossed aside like a piece of meat doesn't it?" Rayne asked in a raised tone and was caught off guard by the slap across the face she received from Lark who turned and ran out of the dressing room. *'I guess she finally go it.'* Rayne thought, tasting blood from biting her tongue when Lark slapped her. *'Damn, why did I do that?'* Rayne inwardly questioned with anger and regret as tears welled in her eyes. *'I seriously think I'm going to have a breakdown from all of these conflicted emotions I'm having. One minute I love her more than ever and I want her back then the next minute I hate her and can't stand to look at her.'* Rayne thought conflicted and inhaled deeply to calm her nerves.

"Lark, honey. Let me drive you back to the hotel." Sal softly offered with concern as he approached the crying woman after hearing the argument.

"No! Just give me your keys." Lark vehemently refused and demanded, grabbing his keys and walking out of the studio. She had to get away from Rayne. Her head pounded and her heart ached from Rayne's biting words. The truth hurt like hell especially when it came from Rayne. Lark had held out hope that they would reconcile, but there was no chance of that according to Rayne and it devastated her. She wished she could remember what happened that fateful night when she was in bed with the other woman.

Lark had gone over it a million times, but couldn't remember that night. She had a huge surprise anniversary party planned for her and Rayne, but got drunk. No, wasted when she became upset with Rayne who phoned her to tell her she wouldn't be able to make it home. Rayne's job forced her to be away quite frequently and Lark felt like she wasn't there for her so, she got ticked off when Rayne said she wouldn't be able to make it home for their anniversary. She didn't know it at the time but Rayne was on her way home to surprise her. Lark couldn't remember leaving the party or after it until she saw Rayne walk into their bedroom with the other woman sitting next to her naked. *'How could I have done something so stupid even if I was totally out of it?'* She asked for the umpteenth time with no answer coming to her, fumbling to get the key in Sal's car door. Her hands shook uncontrollably and she dropped the keys. Lark began to cry harder and bent down to pick the keys up.

"Rayne!" Lark is leaving with my car!" Sal shouted to get her attention and stop her.

"Fuck!" Rayne shouted annoyed and quickly put her shorts on, and grabbed her shirt, then exited the dressing room in a hurry.

"What the hell is going on?" Sal asked angrily.

"Don't ask." Rayne told him as she ran to the door, but forgot her shoes. She headed back to them when she saw the black van pull up and a man grabbed Lark, pulling her into the van. "Shit!" Rayne yelled and ran out the door. "Lark!" Rayne yelled when she saw Lark struggling with her captors.

"Rayne!" Lark screamed with fear.

IV

Lark's scream of shear terror scared the hell out of Rayne and rocked her to that core as she saw the van pull away. Rayne hurriedly ran towards the rental car and jumped on the hood sliding across it to the other side. She landed and kept an eye on where the van was headed as she quickly opened the door to the car. She put the keys in the ignition revving the engine and screeched the tires when she floored the accelerator to follow the van. Rayne put her seatbelt on and weaved in and out of traffic as she tried to catch up to the van. "Damn, Damn!" She angrily shouted and pounded on the steering wheel, pissed for upsetting Lark to the point of her leaving and now being captured. Nothing else mattered to her now except getting Lark back as she maneuvered the car to keep the van within her sight and without letting them know she was following them. *'I'll never forgive myself if something happens to her. She must be terrified being with those people.'* Rayne thought as anger, guilt and fear for Lark's life consumed her. Rayne checked the bags for her phone and realized she left it at the studio along with everything else of hers. Thankfully, she grabbed her gun before she ran out.

Unfortunately, she couldn't stop to call for help in fear that she would lose the van. Rayne's pulse raced along with her adrenaline and wished they would hurry and get somewhere so she could get to Lark. She could live a miserable existence without Lark in her life as long as she was alive, but she couldn't bare the thought of Lark being dead. *'That I can not take,'* She thought as her heart quickened and felt a lump form in her throat at the thought of Lark being dead. She noticed the van turn off down a deserted road and noted that the road was hidden on both sides by a vineyard. She waited for the van to get farther down the dirt road before she attempted it so they wouldn't see the dust cloud from her car. Rayne turned the car down the road slowly when it was safe and she stopped the car to look down the road the van turned down. She saw it parked at an abandoned house and backed the car into the brush to hide it as she grabbed her gun from the seat. She slipped the gun into her waistband and stepped out of the car realizing she had no shoes on. *'Great! It just got worse!'* She thought with a chuckle at the humor of it despite the situation. She slipped the shirt on over her head as she made her way through the vineyard toward the house. *'On the bright side, I'll be able to run faster without shoes.'* She laughed and checked the clip in her gun to make sure she had a plentiful supply of ammunition.

"Ow! Damn it!" Rayne exclaimed when she stepped on a rock with her bare feet. *'I hate walking barefoot!'* She exclaimed and laughed at the memory of Lark hiding her shoes when they were on vacation in Key West. Rayne hated to walk barefoot on any surface except carpeting and the feeling of the dirt surface grossed her out.

In Key West their suite was all tile, no carpeting. One morning before she woke up, the one and only time Lark was up before her, Lark hid her shoes so she would purposely have to walk around the suite barefoot. She laughed at the thought of Lark laughing hysterically until she picked her up kicking and screaming for a thorough dowsing in the cold pool, fully clothed. *'Oh, was Lark pissed.'* She fondly thought with a smile. She got the best end of the deal, when she became extremely aroused by the sight of Lark's perky body showing through her wet, white translucent sundress. She remembered their glorious afternoon of making love, which merged into the evening much to her delight. All was definitely forgiven between the two of them then. Rayne wanted to forgive Lark now, but it was extremely hard for her. Rayne had only trusted one other person as much as she did Lark with her heart, and that woman died in an automobile accident. She loved and trusted the woman completely and thought she was her soul mate, but it was not to be as her world was shattered when Karen passed away.

After her death, Rayne became callous, cold and withdrawn from life, going from one brief sexual encounter with women to another never giving her heart to anyone until Lark entered her life. Rayne tried to avoid falling in love with Lark, but it was no use. The younger blonde beauty captured her heart with her gorgeous green eyes and her fabulous personality. Lark's sexy smile melted Rayne's heart every time she flashed it, and she knew there was no denying the fact that she fell in love with her the moment she first saw her. *'It was fun playing hard to get.'* Rayne thought with a mischievous smile and then sadly said, "Aah yep, that was then and look at where we are now." She found an area where she could slip through the vineyard into the house unnoticed and headed that way.

Lark woke with a killer headache and sat up feeling dizzy. She wrapped her arms around her legs and held her long, blonde hair back off her face with her hand. *'What in the hell happened and where am I?'* She wondered trying to remember and scanned the small room. All she could remember was being pulled into the van and a hand covering her face with a rag containing a strong, horrid smell and then darkness.

Lark surmised that the rag must have contained chloroform, which knocked her out. *'Where are you Rayne?'* She asked silently as her fear consumed her and she began to cry. She wondered if Rayne would come for her. *'Why would she after what I did to her?'* Lark contemplated and wanted to believe she would come for her, but couldn't blame her if she didn't. She thought back to their last conversation and how Rayne's words cut her straight through the heart. Lark had never believed anything like this would happen between them. They loved and trusted each other completely until she turned to another. Now, she worried Rayne would hold that against her and not come for her. *'No, she's too stubborn and too much of a fighter to not come for me.'* Lark reasoned, trying to talk herself into believing she would rescue her.

Lark thought back to the time she first saw Rayne and she knew she was in love the moment that tall, dark and very sexy Secret Service Agent stood next to her father as his protection after an assassination attempt. A smile crept across her face as she remembered seeing her for the first time. *'She was so gorgeous. Hell, she still is but oh, did she sweep me off my feet the moment I looked into those sexy blue eyes.'* Lark reminisced fondly of that time.

Rayne was assigned to protect her father for many years passing off as his aide so she could keep her undercover status. Lark fought hard to get Rayne to go out with her and Rayne fought harder, but Lark won out when Rayne finally agreed to a date. Lark remembered the date as if it were yesterday when she invited Rayne to 'The Melting Pot', her favorite restaurant for fondue. She found it quite adorable that Rayne was nervous for their first date. She looked at Rayne as this strong, tough Secret Service Agent, and she was extremely nervous about their date. After a few minutes at the restaurant her nervousness and shyness left her and she was more relaxed. Lark knew that she had finally found her soul mate in Rayne from their first date. They just clicked with one another and she felt so at ease with Rayne.

On their first month anniversary Rayne told Lark she had fallen in love with her from the moment she saw her, but was afraid to give her heart to another after what happened with her previous girlfriend. She feared the same would happen to Lark and that, she just would not be able to deal with it, she told Lark with tear filled blue eyes.

'Rayne took a huge chance by giving me her heart and I ripped it out. How could I have done that to her?' Lark questioned and began to cry harder at the thought of what she had done to Rayne. *'I have never and I will never love another so completely as I do Rayne. She's my soul mate, she's everything to me and without her love in my heart my life is nothing.'* Lark thought sadly laying her head in her hands and cried harder.

Rayne slipped into the garage area quietly and she quickly dispatched one of the guards knocking him unconscious. She was having a more difficult time with another. She kicked him in the chest and he lost his balance falling backward on a pitchfork, which lay strewn in the garage. Rayne approached the dead man and looked as she passed him. *'Ooh, that's gotta hurt.'* She thought to coldly, heading towards the next room and was greeted by gunfire.

She ducked behind the corner of the wall and slipped her arm around to return the gunfire. She heard the man say something with an accent, which was unrecognizable to her, but she figured he was alerting someone as to what was going down on a walkie-talkie. By the tone of his voice it sounded she figured he had to be asking for help. Rayne jumped, tucked and rolled across the floor before landing on her knees for a better shot, firing her weapon and killing the man.

Lark heard the gunfire and stood up with a smile knowing it had to be Rayne. The door burst open and the leader grabbed her and forcibly pulled her out of the room. "Seems someone likes you and has come to rescue you." The leader angrily told her as he drug her into the living room and covered Lark's mouth with his hand. Lark struggled to break free to alert Rayne of the impending danger to no avail.

Rayne quietly searched different rooms with no luck until she peeked her head into the living room and saw the man holding Lark. Her heart pounded with fear when she saw Lark in the clutches of that man. She fought hard to remove her emotions for Lark so she could concentrate on getting them out of there, alive. She readied her gun holding it out in front of her with it aimed directly at his head. "Seems I have something you want." The leader replied with a smirk.

"Let her go and I promise to only maim you instead of killing you." Rayne sarcastically snapped back. *I could kill him in one second if Lark could move her head to the right.* Rayne thought as she focused on the man, waiting for her opportunity to do just that.

The leader put his gun to Lark's head and laughed. "Drop your gun or I drop her, then you!" He maniacally demanded.

The lump in Rayne's throat grew larger almost cutting off her breathing and her heart raced faster as he held the gun to Lark's head. Rayne re-aimed and squeezed the trigger slightly, hoping to get the opening she needed, but backed off when she saw the terror in Lark's green eyes. She didn't want to take a chance of

91

Lark flinching and taking the bullet instead of the man. She lowered her gun defeated and saw Lark begin to cry in fear that Rayne was their last hope.

Three men ran into the room. "Get her!" The leader angrily demanded and one man hit Rayne in the back of the head with the butt of his gun introducing her to darkness.

Lark struggled and moved her mouth away from the man's hand. "Rayne!" She shouted tearfully when she saw Rayne drop to the ground in a heap.

"Take her back!" He shouted and shoved Lark forward into the arms of another assailant who led her out of the room.

The men tied Rayne to a chair and put smelling salts underneath her nose to wake her. She woke in a hurry and jerked her head away from the foul odor opening fiery blue eyes. The lightness was met by a backhand across the face stinging her cheek. "Thanks, may I have another?" Rayne asked sarcastically and was rewarded with a fist in her face, knocking her back in the chair. *'Fuck, that hurt!'* She thought, feeling the blood trickle from her nose and her eye beginning to swell. *'I'll have to remember to give him a slow painful death.'* Rayne thought maniacally as the chair was propped back up and she looked at the leader with a sly grin. "Is that the best you've got?" She mockingly asked with a grin.

"Don't try me bitch!" He shouted with another slap to her face.

Rayne tasted blood in her mouth and spit it out at his feet and looked up with a grin. "I can do this all day if you want? But unfortunately, my colleagues wouldn't be too happy having to wait for me for that long to report back."

"What?" The leader nervously and angrily asked.

"You heard me I don't stutter! I have fifteen minutes to report back before they storm this joint!" Rayne yelled at him hoping he'd believe her and give up. She didn't think they would, but it was worth a shot.

The man grew more nervous and agitated as he barked out orders to his men they were leaving. "We'll have to make the call from the other location to the rich bitch's daddy. He will sway his vote in favor of the troops leaving Kosovo or risk never seeing his daughter again. I don't know whom they think they are invading our country, but they need to get the hell out! That is our country and we should decide how it will be run not by outsiders who come in and try to destroy country." The leader passionately spoke to one of his men.

'Bite me! It backfired. This guy is a real scumbag to even think that it's right for his country to do ethnic cleansing on his own countrymen.' She thought with increased hate for the man as she struggled to loosen the rope that held her hands. The leader saw her struggling and walked over, hitting her across the face, knocking her out again.

The leader brought Lark into the living room and she struggled to break free when she saw Rayne whose head hung down with her chin nearly touching her chest. Her raven hair was hanging forward over her face shadowing Rayne's features and she feared that Rayne was dead. Her fear consumed her and she broke into tears as she shouted, "Rayne!" before crying harder, desperately trying to break free.

Rayne heard the fear filled voice of the woman she loved so much and struggled to wake up. "Lark!" She responded weekly, attempting to lift her head up and open her eyes.

"Rayne!" Lark yelled happy that she was alive, but concern that she was hurt. She struggled more when she saw her lover move. "Let go of me!" She vehemently demanded as Rayne was finally able to keep her head up and her eyes open. She smiled weakly, knowing the captor was fighting a losing battle by trying to hold Lark back.

Lark looked at the man then back at Rayne who knew what she was about to do. She had taught Lark some self-defense moves and knew what she was thinking. Lark had become quite good with her moves and one day caught Rayne unguarded under the chin sending her to the hospital for five stitches. Lark felt very guilty but she teased Rayne incessantly about it. She made sure she kissed her scar every chance she would get, which Rayne found to be incredibly sweet. Rayne refocused her thoughts from that time to the present and stared into her green eyes with concern and shook her head "no" then mouthed, "Please don't." Rayne hoped Lark would listen to her and not give him an elbow to the mouth like she had taught her to do. She feared he would kill her if she did that and weren't successful with knocking him out.

"Hurry up and get that crap together!" He shouted at his men who worked fervently to get the bomb set up.

Rayne was relieved to see Lark saw the concern in her eyes and did as she asked to do nothing. Lark looked at the leader, "Please let me say goodbye," she pleaded as the tears streamed down her face.

He looked the actress over and agreed to allow her to talk to Rayne. "You've got two minutes." He told her, releasing the grip on Lark who ran to Rayne.

She straddled her on the chair and held her tight as Rayne thought about how good it felt with Lark wrapped around her. "Hey baby! Fancy meeting you here." Rayne whispered teasingly trying to calm Lark down as she sobbed. Lark chuckled and leaned back, locking greens with blues. She cried harder as she pushed Rayne's hair off her face and wiped the blood off her lip as it continued to drip down from her nose. "I think I like this position Lark. We should have tried this before." Rayne joked as Lark laughed, but cried harder at the realization she was about to lose Rayne forever.

"This isn't funny Rayne. This is serious." Lark told her through her tears.

"Aah, this is nothing. I've been in worse situations than this babe." Rayne tried to answer reassuringly, but that was a lie, she had never faced any situation like this before. Well, except in training for the Secret Service, but that was pretend. She didn't want Lark any more upset than she already was so she tried to lighten the mood with her wisecracks. "Please, don't cry baby. You know I can't stand to see you cry."

"There are so many things I need to tell you Rayne." Lark replied regretfully as the tears flowed harder.

"You don't need to. You just told me everything I needed to know with your eyes. Exactly how much you love me." Rayne answered calmly with a loving smile.

"Rayne, I hope you still love me." Lark asked hopeful as she held Rayne's face in her hands and locked her cloudy green eyes with Rayne's calming blues.

"I never stopped loving you Lark and I never will." Rayne wholeheartedly professed with an endearing smile with Lark finding love and sincerity in her blue eyes.

Lark ran her fingers through Rayne's sweaty raven hair and smiled through her tears. "I love you so much Rayne. I'm so sorry." Lark proclaimed, pressing her lips against Rayne's and sought entrance with her tongue, which Rayne gladly accepted. She loved Rayne more than life itself and wanted her to know it through that one kiss.

Rayne felt Lark's love for her through the kiss and wanted Lark to feel hers by reciprocating the kiss and deepening it. Their kiss was interrupted by one of the captors grabbing Lark by the arm. "Let's go time's up." He demanded as Lark shrugged him off and wrapped her arms around Rayne's neck tightly.

"Rayne, I don't want to leave you." Lark cried in a whisper.

"You have to baby. Please, go." Rayne pleaded with Lark hoping she would listen to her.

"No, I can't lose you again. I don't want to live without you. I'm staying here." She demanded and locked her grip while the man tried to break the grip unsuccessfully.

"Babe, have you forgotten already that I'm a contortionist?" Rayne whispered in her ear.

Lark leaned back and looked into Rayne's blue eyes and searched them for reassurance that she would be able to break free, which she found. Lark lovingly smiled as she lightly rubbed her thumb against Rayne's cheek while staring into the blue eyes that she loved so much. She remembered how they would play fight and no matter how many times she thought she had Rayne pinned she would always break free somehow. She smiled as she remembered the many sexual positions they tried which, she was convinced, only a contortionist could have pulled off. "Do you promise to whisk me away on a vacation to Greece if I come and rescue you from these assholes?" Rayne asked with a sexy smile and looked into Lark's beautiful green eyes for possibly the last time.

Lark's tears flowed harder and she laughed at Rayne's arrogance. "I promise." She whispered and sniffled back her tears.

"Lark, I love you." Rayne declared as her heart pounded with fear that she might not ever be able to tell her that again. She lovingly looked at Lark and leaned in to seal the declaration with a soul-searing kiss.

Two captors broke Lark's grip and pulled her away from Rayne as they headed to the door. Lark locked her greens with Rayne's blues hoping she'd be able to look into them again. Rayne smiled to calm the fear she saw in Lark's eyes despite the fact that she was scared as she watched them exit the door. "You shouldn't have killed my brother bitch. Now, you shall find out what it's like to die." The leader shouted with a laugh as he followed everyone out the door.

Rayne struggled with the knot that had her wrists bound, as the clock on the bomb seemed to tick off double time every time she looked at it. Rayne was fortunate that she had hyper mobility in her wrists and was able to contort her wrists enough to slip one out. "Yes!" Rayne exclaimed, turning to untie the other wrist and then her feet. She glanced back at the clock to see it ticked down to 10 seconds. "Fuck, I'm not going to make it!" She shouted and ran for the closest window, diving through it.

Lark heard the blast as they pulled farther away from the house, letting out a blood-curdling scream, "Rayne!" She began to cry as her heart pounded with fear and she sunk down against the seat. The pain she felt in her heart for losing Rayne again was too much for her and she wanted to die to join her soul mate in their afterlife. Lark was happy that she was able to tell Rayne that she loved her and to hear Rayne say it to her. *'I just don't want to go on without her.'* Lark tearfully thought crying harder and thought of everything she loved about Rayne. She loved her blue eyes and how they made her feel complete when they looked at her, her wonderful personality, her arrogance, which she found to be very sexy, and her stubbornness. Lark's thoughts trailed off as she thought about her stubbornness and had renewed hope knowing that Rayne was too stubborn to go out like that. She smiled as her emotions calmed and she didn't have that awful feeling of Rayne being dead. *'She made it out. I know it.'* Lark thought trying to convince herself of that fact.

Rayne crashed through the glass window, landed on her side and rolled to break the impact of the fall. "Aah!" She shouted out in pain from the glass that penetrated her skin, and got up to run to be clear of the impending explosion. "Shit!" She yelled when the pain of the glass in her body pressed against her, especially the piece in her right foot, which increased her pain as she tried to run.

The bomb exploded sending her to the ground from the blast. She struggled to collect her breath when the wind was knocked out of her from the impact of the fall. She tried not to panic knowing that it would eventually come back which it did fairly soon, much to her delight. Rayne sat up and pulled the small piece of glass out of her foot receiving instant relief. She took her shirt off and found a bigger piece of glass deeply imbedded in her side. She decided it was best to leave it right were it was, knowing she could bleed to death if she removed it. She tore her shirt and wrapped part of it around her foot that bled profusely despite the small size of the cut. Rayne took the other part of her shirt and held it to her side where the piece of glass penetrated out from to stop the bleeding. Rayne stood up and headed towards the car as quickly as she could despite her injuries. She was grateful that she didn't feel too much pain, yet and figured it was probably from her adrenaline pumping.

Rayne wondered how she was going to find Lark and figured the best place to start would be at headquarters where the two assailants were being held for interrogation. 'I'll get them to talk, one way or another.' She confidently thought as she reached the car much to her relief.

Rayne sped the car down the dusty road until she found a phone and alerted her Director to the events that took place this evening. He told her he would inform the local office that she was Agent in charge and for them to cooperate with her in anyway possible. She thanked him and hung up the phone before heading back to the car for her trip to the local headquarters.

She grabbed her badge and headed into the large government building and received some very odd looks from the employees as she entered the building. The employees had never had someone enter looking so bloodied and haggard and their faces showed the shock that they felt. The guards moved to stop her thinking she might be a criminal and when she flashed her badge they backed off. "Don't even think about it." She angrily warned, limping towards the front counter. "Where's the Director's office?" She asked with urgency.

"Aah, Director Cady's office is down that hall." The secretary told her, stunned at the sight of Rayne's bloody body and pointed for Rayne's directions.

"Rayne!" A familiar voice shouted from down the hall.

Rayne turned to see Danielle approaching her and was very relieved to see her. "What the hell happened?" She asked concerned and put Rayne's arm around her neck to help her down the hall to the clinic were fortunately, the doctor was on the premises for employee physicals.

"I got too intimate with a bomb." Rayne answered sarcastically.

"Why didn't you call me before you left?" Danielle asked somewhat agitated for being left out of the loop.

"I had to," Rayne attempted to explain, but was interrupted by Danielle.

"You had to make sure I wasn't the insider right?" Danielle asked as she stopped at the door and looked at Rayne disappointed, but with understanding.

"Look Danielle. I'm sorry. I had to check everyone." Rayne answered with regret when she saw the hurt in Danielle's hazel eyes.

"I thought you knew me better than that Rayne, but I understand. I probably would have done the same thing too." Danielle slyly grinned and opened the door, helping Rayne into the clinic.

"I don't have time for this Danielle. I need to see the director and find Lark." Rayne refused agitated by the delay in finding Lark and tried to leave, but was unable to as Danielle held her tighter and led her into the examining room. She helped her up on the table and shouted for the nurse to get the doctor.

Danielle grabbed a cotton ball with alcohol on it and began to wipe the dried blood off of Rayne's face. "You don't have to do that Danielle." Rayne told her, staring at the attractive curly blonde, but really didn't mind the attention.

"I know, but I want to." Danielle answered with a sly smile. "By the way, your insider is Hazel." She informed her and continued to work on her facial wounds.

"I had a strong suspicion that it was her. How did you know?" Rayne asked, disappointed with the formerly faithful employee of Lark's. She knew that Lark would be hurt to find out she was involved.

"Director Bailey faxed the results to Director Cady and he told me when I got here to continue the interrogation." Danielle explained and threw the cotton ball away. She looked over Rayne's wounds thoroughly enjoying Rayne's closeness. She had always been very attracted to Rayne and had hoped that something might happen between the two of them even before Lark and her broke up. *'Who am I fooling? I'm in love with Rayne.'* Danielle inwardly thought and shifted her hazel eyes up to meet with blues.

"Do you still love her?" She asked boldly yet nervous about Rayne's answer.

"Why would you ask me that?" Rayne asked, confused.

"Because of this." Danielle softly answered and pressed her lips agai~st Rayne's for a sensual kiss. She couldn't resist the temptation any longer and had to feel Rayne's lips against her own.

Rayne was stunned that Danielle felt that way about her. *'The kiss was nice, very nice in fact.'* She thought as a mental image of

Lark popped into her head and she broke the kiss. They looked at each other with surprise.

"Rayne, I love you." Danielle confessed as she tucked her long blonde hair behind her ear.

Rayne was shocked. "Aah, Danielle." She stammered nervously as her heart raced and she didn't know what to say. She was saved when the doctor walked in the room.

Danielle stepped back slightly embarrassed. "I'll just be outside." She told her and attempted to leave. *That went over well...not! Who am I fooling? She wants Lark, that's evident.'* Danielle disappointedly thought.

"Danielle, wait! It's okay, you don't have to leave." Rayne answered nervously. She didn't want Danielle to make such a profession and then just walk away before she had a chance to straighten it out, that she wasn't interested in Danielle in sexual way.

Danielle was relieved she wanted her to stay and walked back to the table. "Can we talk about this some other time?" Rayne asked trying to settle the situation for the moment. She had found Danielle to be very attractive, but never really had an interest in her other than friends. "I would like that." Danielle answered with a smile and relief that she wasn't refused right away.

"Great! Can you arrange some clothes for me please?" Rayne asked with a smile and wondered how she had gotten into this mess with Danielle as the doctor attended to the wound on her foot.

"Sure, let me make a call." She suggested and headed to the phone, making a call to have some clothes delivered for Rayne.

The doctor moved his examination up to Rayne's abdomen and delicately removed the piece of glass, which posed no threat to Rayne. "This may need to be looked at by a plastic surgeon."

"Whatever doc. Just sew it up the best you can and I'll have it looked at another time." Rayne hurriedly told him and stood up when the director entered the room. "Hello sir."

"Agent Donovan pleased to meet you. Please sit down." He instructed her with a shake of his hand while he looked over her wounds as the doctor began to suture the wounds.

"It's okay. I have no time. I'd like to speak with the men being held, sir." She requested eager to get some information out of them so she could rescue Lark.

"Aah sure. Doesn't that hurt?" He asked in amazement that she hadn't winced once and the doctor was nearly finished suturing the wound.

"No, I blocked the pain out I guess." Rayne casually explained as an aide brought in clothes for Rayne to wear. Rayne felt very uneasy around Danielle now and needed to push those thoughts out of her head to concentrate on the task at hand. *'Could this whole thing get anymore complicated?'* Rayne queried inwardly, hoping it would not.

"I'll have them brought into the interrogation room while you dress." Director Cady told her on his way out the door.

"Okay, thanks." Rayne answered, looking down and noticing the doctor finished attending to her wounds.

"Agent Donovan I recommend you get these taken care of by a plastic surgeon very soon and here's some pain medication." The doctor advised her and handed her the medication.

"No thanks. I can't have medication dulling my senses especially if I have to use my gun, which seems like it will be the

102

case." Rayne told him, slipping out of her bloody clothing and into a black T-shirt, black fatigue pants and black boots. She grabbed the remaining items and headed out the door, as she would put those on later.

She approached the interrogation room in a very bad mood as her adrenaline and anger pumped. She walked with a slight limp from the boot pressing on the cut on her foot and entered the room to find Danielle questioning the very nervous suspect. Rayne holstered her gun as she watched Danielle question the man and realized she was getting nowhere. "Hey, Danielle. Can I talk to you for a minute?" Rayne asked and nodded her head towards the door indicating she wanted to talk with her privately.

Danielle looked up and smiled when she saw Rayne standing by the door waiting for her with her arms crossed over her chest with and an intimidating look on her face. "Sure, what's up?" She asked as she approached, knowing that Rayne wanted to stall and make the guy more nervous.

Rayne turned her back to the suspect and moved closer to Danielle to speak with her much to Danielle's delight. "Getting nowhere huh?" She asked with a sly smile.

"Yep, in a hurry." Danielle answered with a returned smile.

"Well, maybe I need to scare the little prick huh?" Rayne asked with a maniacal chuckle, changed her look to one of anger and looked over her shoulder at the man who locked eyes with her, indicating to Rayne he was very nervous. Rayne turned back to Danielle with a mischievous grin. "I think he's going to start singing like a bird. Can you step out and let me talk to him alone?" She asked with a smile and a wink.

"Don't scare him too bad because I don't want to have to clean up a mess in that chair." Danielle teasingly laughed and left the room.

Rayne laughed under her breath as she watched Danielle leave the room. *'Let's see if I can cause a code brown with this guy.'* Rayne thought mischievously referring to scaring the shit out of him. Hence, code brown. Rayne pulled out her gun and pulled the clip out pretending to check her supply of ammunition and then replaced the clip. She holstered her gun and looked at the man with piercing blue eyes. Rayne laughed inwardly knowing she had him nailed.

"Hello, I'm Agent Donovan and your worst nightmare." Rayne spoke with sarcastic anger in her voice as she approached the table and looked down at him. She placed her palms on the table and leaned forward bracing herself with her arms making eye contact with the man. She saw the man gulp hard and his body tensed as she looked at him. "Where are your buddies hiding?"

"I...I... don't know." He stammered nervously and was unable to maintain eye contact with Rayne.

"I can see you want to do this the hard way, which is the way I prefer it actually." Rayne answered in a sardonic tone and flashed a mischievous smile as she stood up and slowly walked behind the man.

He nervously glanced over his shoulder at her when she grabbed him behind the neck tightly pushing him forward. "Now, look here ass face! You are going to tell me what I want to hear. You got that?" She angrily and loudly asked, leaning down to his ear.

"What's in it for me?" He asked nervously as he was near tears.

"Let's see. How about if I let you live? You see this is the Secret Service and we have our ways of eliminating people without a trace." Rayne lied to scare him into a confession.

"Aah, you wouldn't?" He asked anxiously and winced from the pain of Rayne's hand gripped on the back of his neck.

"Try me. Now are you going to tell me what I want to hear or should I eliminate you and offer your buddy a better deal?" Rayne answered agitated with his reluctance to tell her what she wanted to hear and squeezed his neck harder.

"Okay, okay, but I want immunity." He nervously demanded as Rayne eased up on her grip.

"Write the directions down to where I can find them and I'll see what I can do for you." Rayne told him and relinquished her hold on his neck and stood up.

"I need a guarantee." He shouted back as Rayne grabbed his neck again and pushed his face down to the paper on the table.

"I said I would see what I could do now write! If your directions are the right one's you'll get your immunity and if they aren't well, you don't want to know what will happen, but I can tell you this that it would involve my gun." She threatened as he began to write the directions down.

Rayne released her grip on the man and stood behind him looking over his shoulder at the directions. "This is one of the planned safe houses we had set up in case something happened. It would be their first choice to hide out in." He explained as he finished the directions.

Rayne reached over and took the paper before slapping him in the back of the head. "Thanks dickhead. I thought you would see it my way!" She replied with a chuckle hurrying to the door and was met by a guard when she opened the door. "Get that piece of shit out of here." She ordered as Danielle and Director Cady approached her.

"Good job agent." The director replied with happiness.

"Thank you sir. I'll need a team of eight with one team of four entering from the front, the other team with three entering from the back and one man to stay back at the van to call in case we need re-enforcements." Rayne instructed him.

"No problem. Danielle can lead one and you the other." He suggested and motioned for his assistant. "Get six more men fully equipped in the basement now." He ordered as his assistant dialed the phone to fulfill his orders.

Danielle and Rayne headed to the basement to meet the rest of the team. "Danielle, you and your team follow me." Rayne instructed her and hopped in the black van.

"Gotcha and Rayne. Be careful." Danielle answered with a smile.

"You too." Rayne answered back as she closed the van door. "Hit it Tom!" She instructed her teammate whom she had worked with many times in the past before he was transferred to the west coast. She was happy he would be assisting on her team. Rayne put on her black fatigue jacket and her headset with a microphone to communicate with everyone else.

"Testing, Danielle do you read?" She asked through the microphone and heard her response indicating the radios were working correctly. She readied the semi-automatic weapon a team member handed her ensuring the weapon would work properly.

She looked up and saw that they were drawing near the location on the map. "Okay Tom. Stop here, we'll have to hoof it the rest of the way for a sneak attack." She instructed him.

"Got it." He answered and stopped the van with everyone exiting to find Danielle was already waiting for them.

"How'd you get here so damn fast?" Rayne asked with bewilderment and disbelief that she didn't notice they weren't following them. '*I have got to be more observant. These distractions should not interfere with the task at hand.*' She chided herself for not concentrating harder on the mission, but thoughts of Lark clouded her mind.

"I saw the location on the map and remembered this place being in this area so, I figured this was the location. I grew up in this area so I know my way around her pretty good." Danielle explained.

"You're lucky you were correct and it was the right one." Rayne answered slightly agitated that she could have gotten lost and for not following her orders. "Move out!" Rayne called out and everyone approached the house through the cover of the trees and the darkness. Rayne motioned for Danielle's team to take the rear as her team waited until they were in place.

Rayne scanned the house with her night vision goggles, indicating three gunmen in the front of the house in the living room area and two in separate front rooms upstairs.

"Falcon two in place." Danielle's voice replied in Rayne's headset.

"10-4. How many do you see?" Rayne asked.

"Two in kitchen, two in a back room." Danielle advised her.

"I have three in the living room, two in separate rooms upstairs, copy?" Rayne asked.

"Affirmative." Danielle answered.

"Okay, let's move in." Rayne ordered as they quietly approached the house. "Ready? Move in." Rayne instructed, and her team slipped into the house through an unoccupied window.

Once her team was in she ordered Danielle's team to move in and use radio silence to prevent them from tipping the people in the house off. Rayne used hand signals to motion her team members to their destinations. Three were to take the men in the living room and she was heading upstairs to find Lark and to take out the men up there. Danielle's team slipped in a side window unnoticed and she ordered her men to take the two in the kitchen and for one member to join her in the back bedroom to take out the assailants there. Rayne silently moved upstairs trying to keep her breathing calm to slow her racing heart down. She could hear Lark pleading with her captor to let her go. It pained her too much to have to hear her pleading for her life and she could hear the fear in her voice, which made her heart race faster. *'I'm right here baby. I'm coming for you.'* Rayne said, wishing Lark could hear her and deduced they were in the back bedroom. She slipped down the hall to take out the lone gunman in the other room. *'He was too easy or I'm too good.'* She arrogantly thought with a chuckle as she tied up the unconscious man. *'Probably the latter.'* She cockily gloated.

She heard gunfire erupt downstairs and hurried to the door. She peeked out the door to find the leader had Lark in his grasp with a gun pointed at her. He looked down the stairs and shouted, trying to find out what was happening. He didn't see Rayne slowly approach him from the side. She saw the fear and shock in Lark's emerald green eyes as if she had seen a ghost when Rayne stepped out of the bedroom. She focused greens on blues and felt less fearful now that she knew Rayne was there and she was alive. Lark was so happy with the latter that she began to cry and the man turned to tell her to shut up, finding Rayne aiming her gun at him.

"I guess you've got nine lives." He smirked at Rayne.

"Meow." Tauntingly replied. "Now, let's make sure you only have one." Rayne answered conceitedly with a sly grin.

"You won't shoot me with your bitch so close to me!" He laughed as he moved to position his gun to Lark's head and Rayne fired her gun at him before he got the gun there.

He felt the blast rip through his thigh, "Aah!" he screamed and writhed on the ground in pain.

Rayne ran over and kicked the gun out of his hand. "I surprised you didn't I ass face?" She tauntingly shouted with a smirk on her face. Lark ran over and wrapped her arms around Rayne sobbing uncontrollably. "It's okay baby. I told you I would come for you." Rayne reassured Lark and held her in her arms, happy that she still had the chance to do so.

"I thought you were dead." Lark cried out.

"I'm too stubborn for that. You should know that better than anyone else." Rayne answered with a chuckle, looking at Lark who lifted her head up and met blue eyes with a smile through her tears.

"I remembered that later, but I worried when it took so long for you to get here." Lark tearfully told her and smiled happy that her lover was there.

Rayne smiled and glanced back to see the leader had pulled out another gun before Rayne could ready hers. Rayne pushed Lark out of the way as he fired his gun at Rayne. She felt the bullet hit her, then her breath escaped her and she heard another shot as she felt pain rip through her head before darkness consumed her.

V

Danielle saw the man fire at Rayne as she made her way up the stairs but she was too late to stop him. She wasn't late enough for retribution and shot the man, killing him instantly.

"RAYNE!" Lark screamed in horror as she struggled to get up and rush to Rayne's side, but was cut off by Danielle who beat her to Rayne who lay motionless on the ground with her head against the wall.

"Rayne, baby, no this wasn't supposed to happen." Danielle replied with worry and concern as she checked Rayne over. She opened her shirt to find the bullet had lodged in her bulletproof vest directly over her heart.

"Rayne." Lark cried out fearfully as she knelt beside her wounded lover and began to cry harder when she saw how motionless Rayne looked.

Danielle was unable to find Rayne's pulse and checked to see if she was breathing which she was not. "Lark! Get that vest open!" Danielle shouted with urgency as Lark did as she instructed her to.

Danielle ripped her headset off knowing she was going to have to start CPR and didn't need a hindrance. Danielle slid Rayne's body down on the floor flat and held her nose closed, tilted her head back to blow two breaths into her lungs. Danielle moved her hands down Rayne's chest and positioned them over her sternum to begin chest compressions. She counted off fifteen compressions and put her ear to Rayne's nose to assess her breathing. "Come on baby, breath." Lark nervously coaxed through her tears and squeezed Rayne's hand to let her know she was there for her.

Danielle checked her breathing again. "She's breathing!" Danielle answered with a smile and a sigh of relief, checked her pulse and found a strong one. One of the team members ran up the stairs as Danielle sat up, "Get an ambulance!" she shouted as he nodded in acknowledgement of his orders and radioed the van with the communications team member to call for an ambulance.

Danielle checked Rayne's eyes and pulse before checking for a head wound, which she found after pulling her hand back, which had blood on it. "She must have hit her head when she fell." Danielle surmised as she applied pressure with her hand and sat Rayne up to decrease the swelling in her brain, cradling her in her arms as she sat behind her. " Hold on baby. Help is on its way." Danielle whispered with worry.

Lark moved Rayne's hair off her face and lightly rubbed the back of her hand against her cheek. She pulled Rayne's hand up to her face and lightly kissed the limp extremity. She cried harder as she held Rayne's hand against her cheek. "Come on honey. Don't leave me." Lark pleaded through her tears, as her whole life lay motionless before her. She was worried that Rayne wouldn't make it from the way she looked. Rayne was everything to her and she didn't want to lose her this way. *'I don't want to lose her in any way.'* She thought as her heart pounded with fear of losing Rayne.

Danielle kissed the top of Rayne's head. "It's okay. Help is here." She whispered when she heard the paramedics enter the house while Lark bore a hole through Danielle with her piercing, angry green eyes as to her kissing Rayne. "I performed one cycle of CPR before she began to breathe again and I was able to find her pulse." Danielle informed them as they approached.

"Excuse us!" The paramedics responded as they moved Lark out of the way to examine Rayne. Lark stood out to of the way with worry as she watched the paramedics check Rayne's vital signs, apply an oxygen mask, hook her up to a heart monitor, and started an IV. "Okay, she's got a strong heart beat and a pulse." The paramedic replied as he checked the heart monitor. Once they felt she was stabilized they transferred her onto the stretcher. The paramedics wheeled her down the stairs and out of the house to the ambulance as Lark tried to step in for the ride to the hospital with Rayne, which they would not allow.

"I'm her lover." Lark pleaded to no avail.

"You've hurt her enough Lark." Danielle snapped and stepped into the ambulance. "I'm her partner." She informed them, flashing her badge and closed the doors as the ambulance drove off.

Lark rushed over to the Director who had just arrived on the scene. "Please, you have to take me to the hospital." She cried as the tall man turned to her.

"You're Lark Morgan right?" He asked as Lark nodded yes. "Okay, let's go and you can explain to me what happened on the way." He suggested as they quickly headed to his car and drove off.

Lark wasn't sure if she made any sense when she informed the Director of what she knew regarding the incident that happened in the house because all she could think about was Rayne. He pulled up to the emergency room entrance and Lark was out of the vehicle and into the hospital before the car came to a complete stop.

She rushed in to find Danielle arguing with the nurse at the desk. "I don't care if you're her partner. You're not allowed in there." The nurse snapped back.

"Excuse me. How is Rayne Donovan?" Lark urgently asked when she approached the desk.

"Are you family?" The nurse asked agitated, as Danielle looked on not too pleased that Lark was there.

"Yes, I am. My name is Lark Morgan." She answered out of breath and aggravated with all the questions. She was part of Rayne's family, not Danielle and she was going to make sure that Danielle knew that.

"Oh, yes Miss Morgan we've been trying to contact you. We got your name from Miss Donovan employers and she has you listed as her emergency contact." The nurse answered with an improved demeanor about her. "Follow me the doctor would like to talk to you." She answered with a smile as she led Lark towards the examining rooms, leaving a very agitated Danielle in the waiting room.

"Damn it!" Danielle thought with contempt as she watched Lark being led down the hallway to see Rayne.

"Agent Bridges, we need to debrief you." The Director instructed as he walked up behind Danielle.

"Not now sir." She answered with anger and nervousness.

"No, now! Let's go." He ordered and nudged her towards the door, as Danielle was reluctant to go with him.

The doctor explained that Rayne had a concussion along with a hematoma on her chest from the impact of the bullet and that her previously sutured wounds had reopened. He advised Lark that a plastic surgeon was nearly finished suturing her wounds and that the reason she required CPR was from the force of the bullet hitting the vest causing her heart to stop. He also advised Lark that Rayne would be held for observation and they wanted to make sure she didn't have an epidural hematoma. He ordered a CAT scan to check for the epidural hematoma as a precautionary measure, which he explained in laymen's terms as a skull fracture with the pooling of blood in the dura mater or lining of the brain as he noticed the confusion on Lark's face.

"So, she's going to be okay?" Lark asked with guarded relief.

"She'll be fine just as soon as she wakes up and provided the CAT scan comes back negative for an epidural hematoma which I believe it will. I have found nothing unusual with the EKG that monitors her heart which is very good news." He answered with a reassuring smile.

114

"Oh, thank you doctor. Can I see her please?" Lark asked with excitement and relief as her nervousness calmed slightly.

"Sure, the nurse will show you in." He answered with a smile and motioned for the nurse to show her to where Rayne was sleeping.

The nurse escorted Lark in to the curtained area where Rayne lay peacefully sleeping. She stood just inside the curtain and stared at the love of her life who laid extremely still, *'too still.'* Lark thought worriedly as the tears trickled down her face.

"We are going to take her down for the CAT scan and she'll be moved to her room within forty-five minutes. Talk to her and see if you can get her to wake up." The nurse informed Lark before she stepped out.

Lark stood next to Rayne and lightly brushed the back of her hand on Rayne's cheek as she lovingly looked at her still soul mate. If it weren't for the monitors attached to Rayne signaling a heartbeat she would believe that she was dead she was that motionless.

The rise and fall of Rayne's chest when she would breath was barely noticeable and it scared the hell out of Lark. Lark cried harder at the thought of losing Rayne forever. She could deal with Rayne not being in her life well, somewhat because she would know she was alive and well, but if she was dead well... *'Stop thinking that way, she's alive.'* Lark inwardly reminded, and ran her fingers through Rayne's disheveled raven hair. Lark wished she could trade places with Rayne to take away her pain. *'I owe her my life.'* Lark thought sadly as she wiped away her tears. "Hey, baby. I'm here." Lark whispered through her tears as she leaned down and lightly kissed her cheek. Lark pressed her cheek against Rayne's as the tears flowed freely. "Rayne, wake up honey." She requested coaxingly and held Rayne in her arms. "Please baby its time to wake up."

"I'm sorry. We're here to transport her for the CAT scan." The transport tech replied when he opened the curtain.

Lark looked back startled and nodded in acknowledgement, kissing Rayne's cheek before she stood up wiping away her tears. "I'll be waiting for you in your room Rayne." Lark told her and squeezed her hand before they wheeled her off for her test.

'Lark, can't you hear me?' Rayne asked as she thought she was saying that to her out loud. *'Can't she feel me squeezing her hand? I'm so tired and I feel like I was hit by a train, sleep, I need sleep.'* Rayne thought and drifted off.

Lark called Rayne's brother to let him know what had happened and he informed her he would be there just as soon as he contacted his parents in Greece to let them know also. She called Elaine to inform her of the turn of events so she wouldn't go out of her mind looking for her. Elaine assured her she would handle the media if word got out of the incident and would come to the hospital tomorrow. Lark also called Director Cady to let him know of Rayne's status. She waited anxiously in Rayne's room and was relieved when they wheeled her in into the room.

Lark sat next to Rayne in a chair and held her hand. "Hey, sleepyhead it's time to wake up. Are you going to sleep all night?" She teased and ran her fingers through Rayne's hair. Lark's heart skipped a beat every time she looked at the cuts and bruises all over Rayne's body. Her chest tightened along with her throat at the pain Rayne endured for her. She went through total hell for her and she owed Rayne her life, plus more. Lark's guilt consumed her and she covered her face with her hands and sobbed at the pain she has caused Rayne. "I'm so sorry Rayne for everything. I love you so much and I don't ever want to be away from you. I want us to be together again without your love in my heart my life is nothing." She sobbed harder and laid her head down on Rayne's lap. "Maybe I don't deserve your love Rayne. Maybe you would be better off without me." Lark cried harder at the confused thought, as she wasn't making sense through her grief.

Rayne was finally able to open her eyes, but found it hard to focus. She turned her head to see a familiar blond figure lying in her lap crying, albeit, it was blurry, but she knew it was Lark. She smiled happily knowing that Lark was alive and well. "I'd be better off without the crying." She teased through a whisper and reached to softly stroke Lark's blond hair.

Lark thought she imagined she heard Rayne's voice until it was confirmed by her touch. She turned her head around quickly and smiled when she saw Rayne's stunning blue eyes looking at her. Rayne's hand rested on Lark's cheek and she turned to place a kiss on the palm before moving up closer to her. "Baby, I was so worried about you." Lark admitted and clutched Rayne's hand, kissing it again.

"I know I could hear you." Rayne answered hoarsely. "I heard all the crying too. Didn't you know I was trying to sleep?" Rayne teasingly chuckled as she tried to lighten the mood and focus with more clarity.

Lark laughed through her tears of happiness that fell as she moved closer to Rayne, hoping she wouldn't reject the kiss she wanted to give her. Lark hesitated and searched her blues for acceptance, which she didn't see until Rayne ran her hand through her long blond hair. She placed her hand behind Lark's neck and pulled Lark down to her chest, hugging her as closely as possible without causing herself pain from her tender chest. Lark was disappointed that she didn't get the kiss that she wanted and looked up at Rayne.

Rayne lovingly wiped away Lark's tears with a smile and Lark leaned back down burying her face in Rayne's neck as Rayne hugged her close to her. "I am so sorry for you getting injured to save me." Lark replied and cried.

Rayne kissed her head. "I know you are. Come on, please stop crying you know I can't stand to hear you cry." Rayne pleaded softly, rubbing Lark's back to comfort the sobbing woman. Rayne felt Lark's sobbing calm as she continued to rub her back and held her close taking in the sweet scent so specific to her lover. *'Oh, how I love to feel her in my arms.'* Rayne thought as her own tears slipped down her cheeks. *'Do I have it in my heart to forgive her?'* She asked and snapped out of her thoughts when her brother rushed into the room and she quickly wiped away her tears.

"Rayne!" He exclaimed with excitement to see her awake as Lark sat up and wiped her tears away.

Rayne looked at Lark with a smile and squeezed her hand as her brother hugged her. "You okay?" He asked with concern as his matching blues met Rayne's and he lovingly pushed her hair back off her face.

"Well, other than feeling like I was hit by a train I'm doing okay." Rayne teased with a smile.

Her brother smiled with relief once he was convinced his sister was going to be okay. He looked her over and was overwhelmed by all of the bruises and cuts on his baby sister. "Damn Rayne! What's the other guy look like?" He asked with a sly grin.

"Aah, I'm not sure." Rayne answered with a bewildered look and turned to look at Lark for an answer.

"He's dead." She answered dryly as she looked at Shayan with red eyes and a tear-streaked face.

"I should have known that would be the case if someone tangled with you." He grinned proudly that she was tough from all of his self-defense techniques he taught her growing up so she could take care of herself.

"Well, I don't remember killing him." Rayne answered confused as she held her hands out with her palms up and shrugged her shoulders.

"That's because Danielle did it," Lark answered reluctant to bring up her name, 'and she also saved your life by performing CPR on you." Lark informed them, as she was upset that she had to stand by and not help because she didn't know CPR.

"She did?" Rayne answered with a chuckle. "Where is she anyway? I thought she would be here. I need to thank her." Rayne asked looking between her brother and Lark.

Lark looked down at her hands, sad that Rayne seemed so excited to see Danielle. She felt so inadequate and unwanted. "I'm not sure, but she was talking with the Director when I came in to see you. Aah, I'm going to let the nursing staff know you're up and awake." Lark informed her, feeling more uncomfortable discussing Danielle. She realized Danielle was in love with Rayne and it seemed like Rayne might be interested in her as well.

"Okay, thanks." Rayne answered slightly confused by Lark's demeanor, watching Lark leave the room and looked back at Shayan.

"Is she okay?" Shayan asked with concern.

"Physically yes, but I don't know about emotionally." Rayne answered with concern for her blonde lover.

Lark alerted the nursing staff that Rayne was awake and headed to the cafeteria for a cup of coffee. *'What's Rayne's deal with Danielle?'* Lark inwardly wondered. *'Is she in love with her or just dating her?'* She asked sadly and tormented by her question. Lark hoped that she wasn't in love with Danielle as she sipped the hot beverage and walked back to Rayne's room.

"Okay Rayne I want you to stay awake as much as possible tonight. I didn't see any evidence of a skull fracture on the CAT scan, which is positive news, but your brain has some swelling present."

119

"Great! Just what I want to do for the rest of the night." Rayne answered sarcastically.

"I'll keep you awake." Lark eagerly offered when she entered the room and sat next to Rayne on the bed sipping her coffee.

Rayne smiled and rested her hand on Lark's thigh sending warmth straight to Lark's core from her soft touch. "Thanks, but you don't have to. You look tired. Go ahead and get some sleep." She suggested with a pat on the leg, appreciative of her offer to stay.

"No, I'd rather stay. I can sleep in the chair." She answered, nervously thinking that Rayne didn't want her there. She didn't want to leave in case Danielle showed up. She didn't like the woman and for obvious reasons.

"Lark, you don't have to, really." Rayne answered with a raised eyebrow-knowing Lark was ready to fallout at any moment by the sleepy look in her eyes.

"Rayne, I want to. Please don't make me leave." She pleaded with tears in her eyes and a shaky tone.

"Okay, I'd love the company." Rayne relented with a slight smile and wondered why Lark was so adamant about staying. She knew that Lark never gave up an opportunity to sleep and Rayne found it hard to believe she was going to miss this one.

"Hey, bro. Get back to your family. I'm fine, really." Rayne told him with a smile and a wink.

"Are you sure?" He asked, seeking surety from Rayne.

"Positive and tell mom and dad that they don't need to come back from Greece. I'll be fine." She answered reassuringly.

"I'll call them and tell them to give you a call. They were very worried." He informed her and kissed her on the forehead. "I love you." He whispered in her ear followed by a kiss to the cheek.

Rayne smiled and hugged him, "Ditto," as she released the hug.

He stood up and walked over to Lark. "Take care of our girl." He replied with a kiss to her cheek.

"You can count on it." Lark answered with a smile and watched as he began to walk away.

"Hey, Rayne. I like the shiner you've got." He teased with a wink.

"Is it like the one I gave you when we were kids?" She teased back with a smile.

"I fell on your fist and you know it!" He answered with a laugh and a wave goodbye as he left the room.

Rayne laughed and thought about how much better she felt already. She looked her arms over to see there were small cuts on them from the glass and pulled her gown away from her chest to see the huge hematoma on her chest. "Whoa! That's huge, look." She exclaimed with amazement, looking at where the bullet hit her vest causing the trauma and leaned forward to show Lark who peered down her gown.

"Oh, my god it's huge, and the hematoma too." Lark teased with a laugh referring to Rayne's perky breast that she would love to wrap her mouth around.

Rayne looked up at her and laughed along with Lark. Rayne pulled her gown back to check the wound in her side and found it had been bandaged. Lark couldn't keep her eyes off of Rayne's bare, muscular abdomen not to mention the dark curls that peeked out from underneath the gown. Rayne glanced over and saw the look of lust in her eyes. "Do you see something you like?" She asked mischievously as Lark looked at her with embarrassment and a flushed face, which was turning a crimson color by the minute.

"Well, aah yeah." Lark admitted with a sheepish grin, lowering her head with embarrassment and tucked her long blonde hair behind her ear, something that Rayne found to be very erotic.

Rayne laughed at her shyness and embarrassment. "I can understand your dilemma Lark. I'm sexy, what can I say?" Rayne teased with mock arrogance and a laugh shared by Lark. She slid her foot up towards her to look at the wound on her foot and leaned forward becoming very dizzy.

Lark saw her loss in balance and grabbed her to steady her. "Rayne, are you okay?" She asked and leaned her back against the upright bed.

"Oh, man. I got wicked dizzy. Lark hand me the bedpan, quick! I'm going to get sick." Rayne asked urgently as she gagged and covered her mouth to fight the hyperemesis.

Lark grabbed the bedpan and handed it to her as Rayne barely got it to her mouth before becoming very sick. Lark looked on with concern and went into the bathroom to wet a washcloth and returned as Rayne finished. Rayne lay against the pillow breathing deeply to calm her nausea.

"Feeling better?" Lark asked with concern and lovingly wiped Rayne's face off with the washcloth.

Rayne stared into Lark's green eyes and thought about how much she loved the attention Lark was giving her. She wanted that compassion from Lark six months ago when she was upset about the tragic deaths of her grandmother and partner. Rayne put her hand on Lark's who stopped wiping her face and shifted her green eyes to meet blues. "Lark, why couldn't you have been this caring months ago when I needed you?" Rayne asked softly, searching her eyes for an answer.

Lark looked down at the hand that lovingly held her own and was regretful as the tears filled her eyes. "Because I was being selfish Rayne. You were withdrawn and I didn't think you loved me or wanted to be with me anymore." She tearfully admitted as her green eyes met confused blues.

Rayne shifted her head to look more directly at her. "Lark how could you think that? I loved you more than life itself." She sincerely asked with disbelief at her confession.

Lark's tears rolled down her cheeks uncontrollably. "I felt like you were pushing me out of your life and when you didn't come home for our anniversary it confirmed my suspicions Rayne. I had a surprise party all set up with our friends and when you called me saying you couldn't make it I was devastated. I just felt like you didn't care enough to come home for our anniversary. So, I got wasted to drown out my pain." She explained crying harder and was glad that at least Rayne could talk with her about it without yelling or being harsh.

Rayne reached up and wiped away Lark's tears that leaned her face against her hand. "Lark, I told you I wouldn't be home because I wanted to surprise you, but it backfired on me when my plane was delayed. I knew about the party and I intended to surprise you by coming there late. I wanted to ask you to be my partner for life. I ended up at the party about fifteen minutes after you left." Rayne explained with sadness at the misunderstandings of that evening.

Lark cried harder as Rayne pulled her down and hugged her. "Rayne, I'm so sorry." She sobbed against Rayne's neck.

"Me too." Rayne whispered and kissed the blonde on her head.

"Can you ever forgive me?" She asked through her sobs.

"I don't know Lark. I just can't get past what happened and I don't know if I can ever look at you without feeling those painful emotions of betrayal and deceit." Rayne admitted trying to sort out her feelings for Lark.

Lark looked up at her. "Do you still love me?" She asked through her tears.

"I always have and I always will Lark you know that." Rayne wholeheartedly reassured her.

"Do you still want me? Or do you want Danielle? I know that she's in love with you." Lark asked with sadness and fear at the thought that Rayne would choose Danielle over her.

Rayne hesitated with her answer and felt overwhelmed like she was being pressured into an answer she may regret giving. "Lark I do still want you, but I don't know if I can forgive you and if I can't do that then we will just continue to hurt each other more. I want to look at you with nothing but love, instead of what I see now, betrayal. I don't want that. There are no feelings on my part for Danielle other than her friendship." Rayne explained and didn't feel like Lark was truly sorry about her indiscretions.

"As much as it hurts Rayne. I understand and I only hope you can find it in your heart to forgive me so you can love me without hesitation or doubt again." Lark answered as the tightness in her chest increased. It wasn't what she really wanted to hear, but she had to give Rayne the time she needed and by what she read from Rayne's blue eyes she knew they would be together again, someday. She was glad that Rayne's feelings for Danielle were on a friendship only basis. "I guess I should leave now and let you rest." Lark suggested and moved to leave.

"No." Rayne retorted, grabbing her hand. "I would rather you stay with me." Rayne admitted as she looked at Lark who was confused.

"I thought you wanted to be alone?"

"I do, but I don't feel comfortable with you leaving by yourself. I still don't have a very good feeling about everything that's happened and I'd rather not be alone tonight and besides, you said you would stay to keep me awake. I'll think about everything tomorrow." Rayne answered with a smile not wanting Lark to leave until she knew everything was cleared up or she could have someone escort Lark home.

"If that's what you want then, I'll stay." Lark answered, wiping her tears away and moved towards the chair.

"You can stay right here." Rayne offered with a smile and patted the bed next to her for Lark to lie there.

Lark's heart skipped a beat at the thought of Rayne holding her in her arms and was confused as to what was going on, but she didn't want to be away from her. She figured if Rayne wanted her to be there it confirmed that what she saw in Rayne's eyes was true that she did still want her or did she misread her?

Lark crawled up in the bed with Rayne and tucked her head in the crook of Rayne's arm, snuggling closer to her and wrapping her arm around Rayne's waist. Rayne gently stroked her long hair, enjoying the feeling of having Lark back in her arms again. Before long she felt Lark's soft breath against her chest and heard her shallow breathing and knew she was fast asleep.

'So much for helping to keep me awake.' She silently laughed and shifted to look at Lark who clutched her arm in desperation for closeness through her sleep. Rayne was taken back by what Lark had done and thought as if Lark was saying, *'please don't leave.'* Rayne lay back in place and kissed Lark's head. She felt Lark's grasp on her arm release in relief that Rayne wasn't going anywhere.

Rayne watched TV and listened to Lark's light snoring throughout the rest of the night; thinking about what she intended to do with this whole situation. She wanted to be with Lark that much was true. She just had to figure out how she was going to do that without looking at Lark with feelings of betrayal and without wondering each time she is around another person if she is having an affair with them. She wanted to make sure she could love and trust her whole-heartedly once again. If she couldn't, then they would be better off without each other in their lives as they would just make each other miserable.

Rayne talking on the phone to her brother Jayce, who Rayne tried to convince that, she was fine awakened lark. Rayne looked at the sleepy blonde next to her and smiled. "Can you talk some sense into him?" She asked hopeful and handed the phone to Lark.

"Jayce, she's fine, don't worry so much." She replied with a laugh at his nervousness after taking the phone.

"Are you in bed with her?" He asked with shock and disbelief.

"Aah yes, I am." She stammered, slightly embarrassed.

"You guys, aah didn't." He stuttered nervously not wanting to just blurt out his question.

"No, we didn't do it in the hospital bed if that's what you're asking." Lark teasingly assured him and heard a sigh of relief from him.

"Good! I was going to be jealous that my sister would be one up on me for unusual places to have sex." He laughed.

"Oh, really?" Lark sarcastically asked. "So, have you done it in first class on an airplane?" She asked with a laugh.

"Lark, give me the phone." Rayne order with shock and embarrassment as she grabbed the phone while Lark and Jayce laughed. " You two need to knock it off." She warned feeling uncomfortable with the conversation.

"Well, what's his answer?" Lark asked with a laugh as she strained to get her ear near the phone to hear his answer. Rayne shook her head no with a mischievous smile. "She's one up on you Jayce!" Lark shouted into the phone with a laugh.

"Yes, little brother. I told you I'm fine! So, I can't talk you out of coming? Okay, be careful then. I love you, bye." She replied and clicked the phone off. "Well, Jayce is on his way out." Rayne informed her, slightly defeated that she didn't convince him she was fine, but she was happy that he was coming. She hadn't seen him since he began his last year of law school at Harvard and missed hanging out with him.

"It will be great to see him again." Lark answered with a mischievous smile.

"What's up with the two of you?" Rayne skeptically asked with a sly grin and a raised eyebrow, looking down at Lark who went back to resting in the crook of Rayne's arm.

Lark laughed. "Nothing." She answered evasively and looked up, seeing that Rayne didn't believe her. "Really, you know his biggest fantasy is to be with two women and I just love to tease him by giving him something to think about."

"He's a dog isn't he?" Rayne asked with a laugh.

"Like someone else I know." Lark teased with a knowing smile, looking at Rayne and tried to get up, but was grabbed by a couple of strong arms and pulled back down. Lark flipped her hair off her face and giggled from Rayne's playfulness.

Lark turned to face Rayne and their eyes locked telling each other what they both felt for one another. Rayne's smile turned serious as she looked at Lark. "You are so beautiful." Rayne whispered once she caught her breath and softly traced Lark's lips with her finger before sitting her back up in the bed as the painful memories came rushing back from that fateful night.

Lark and Rayne looked at one another with an uncomfortable silence as the doctor entered the room. "Miss Donovan, I see you're feeling better." He replied with a smile as he approached the bed while Lark stood up beside it.

Lark couldn't take the mixed messages they were driving her nuts. *'As much as I don't want to I have to stay away until she makes her decision. I can't take getting my hopes any more to only have them squashed if she decides she can't forgive me.'* Lark thought sadly, watching the doctor examine Rayne.

"I have never met someone who has healed from a severe concussion as quickly as you have." The doctor exclaimed with surprise.

"You've never met me before doc, that's why." Rayne cockily answered and laughed.

"Even still. I want another CAT scan done just to be on the safe side and if everything looks good with that and your latest EKC I'll release you later today." He instructed Rayne much to her delight.

"Well, let's get going doc. I've got things to do." Rayne teased, as she was anxious to get the test completed and get out of the dreadful hospital.

"Someone will be in shortly to take you down." He answered with a chuckle and he walked away shaking his head.

"Tom! Hey! Good to see you again." Rayne excitedly exclaimed when her team member Tom entered the room. She was in a great mood considering the latest news, that she would be sprung from the joint not to mention getting out of the hideous hospital gown.

"Rayne, I'm glad to see you're okay. We thought you had a date with the grim reaper." He chuckled and shook her hand.

"Dude, I'm too ornery for that guy. Did you meet Lark?" She asked as she pointed in her direction.

"Aah...no...I...aah...haven't." He stammered timidly at meeting a celebrity. "I saw you at the scene last night but didn't get a chance to meet you. Hello, I'm Tom." He nervously repeated Rayne's introduction as he shook Lark's hand.

"Nice to meet you Tom and thank you for your help. I really appreciate it and if there's anything I could do to thank you, please let me know." Lark answered cordially with an appreciative smile.

He smiled at the thought that a celebrity was so appreciative towards him. "Well, aah there is one thing you could do. The guys and I are big fans of yours and I was wondering if I could get my picture taken with you along with an autograph if that's not too much to ask?" He asked shyly as Rayne snickered behind him.

"I'd be happy to, but I would like to do it when I'm looking a little better if you don't mind?" Lark asked with a smile referring to her haggard look and red eyes from crying.

"Anytime is fine with me. I want the other guys to eat their hearts out." He answered with a laugh.

"I have some free time tomorrow around noon if you can meet me then."

"Unfortunately, I'll be knee deep in paperwork from this latest case at that time." He regretfully answered.

"No problem. I can come down to headquarters with my photographer for the picture and I'll have him develop it, I'll autograph it and send it back to you." Lark explained, as his eyes widened with disbelief that she was so nice and personable to go through all of that for him.

"Excellent, thank you." He answered appreciatively and excitedly, turning to see Rayne laughing at him for his over exuberance with Lark. "Oh, cut it out." He replied embarrassed.

"That's weak man. If you wanted an autograph I could have gotten it for you when we worked together in Florida dude." Rayne answered with a laugh.

"Yeah, but I felt funny asking you to do it and seeing as how she offered it didn't bother me so much."

"What's up with the suspect?" Rayne asked changing the conversation.

"Aah the suspect has been apprehended and is in custody as we speak." Tom answered hesitantly knowing that Hazel was a close friend and employee of Lark's.

"Hey, can you wait outside while I talk to Lark for a minute please?" Rayne asked knowing she should be the one to tell Lark of Hazel's involvement in the whole kidnapping scheme.

"Sure, no problem." Tom answered and lowered his head, heading outside to wait.

"What's going on Rayne? Who's the person on the inside?" Lark asked with worry from Rayne's demeanor and walked to the bed.

Rayne held her hand for comfort. "It's Hazel. I'm so sorry." Rayne sincerely told her seeing the hurt and pain that she was so familiar to in Lark's green eyes.

"No, I can't believe it." Lark answered as the tears flowed and she shook her head in disbelief at the woman's betrayal.

"I'm sorry Lark, but it's true." Rayne softly reiterated and stroked Lark's hand for comfort.

"I can't believe this whole thing. I mean Hazel? I'm totally floored. Why did this whole thing happen to me in the first place?" Lark questioned and began pacing the floor next to Rayne's bed trying to figure everything out.

"I'm not sure what Hazel's motives are, but if I had to guess it would probably be for money, and a lot of it. As far as you being the target, it's because of who your father is and because of who you are. He is the deciding vote to sway Congress either way in the situation with Kosovo and you're a very high profile actress so, they figured you would be the best target to get your father's vote to go in their favor. It's stupid reasoning, but these people do strange things to get what they want." Rayne explained as Lark stood next to the bed and Rayne clasped her hand.

"This is just so unbelievable." Lark softly said, not knowing what else to say. She felt totally betrayed and ran an absent hand through her long hair, frustrated by the turn of events.

"Lark, I'm going to have Tom take you back to the hotel to see that you make it there safely, okay?" Rayne asked and squeezed her hand for comfort.

"Okay, I aah guess I'll talk to you whenever?" She asked Rayne unsure of what she should say or do next regarding their situation.

"Yeah, I'm going to hang out with the boys, Shay, Holly and Jayce for a couple of days while I recuperate. You can give me a call on my cell phone if you want to, here's my new number." Rayne suggested and jotted it down on a piece of paper, handing it to Lark. Rayne looked up at the TV and saw Lark's agent being interviewed by a TV station. She turned the volume up to listen. "Lark, I think the vultures have found out what happened." Rayne replied as she looked up at the TV.

"Is it true that Lark Morgan was killed in the kidnapping attempt?" A reporter asked her agent, Elaine.

"That is totally untrue. She is alive and well." Elaine answered disgusted by the stupid question as she tried to make her way through the crowd from her car. "Lark Morgan will issue a statement in the near future." She informed the reporters and passed by them entering the hospital.

"Great, that means I'm going to be mobbed getting out of here." Lark sighed with disdain at the thought of having to answer a million questions from nosey reporters.

"Well, maybe not. We can get Tom to sneak you out." Rayne informed her to calm her nervousness, which she felt in Lark's hand that shook like a leaf as she held it.

Lark fought the tears that wanted to fall as she looked at Rayne and hoped she would still be a part of her life, sniffing the tears back. "I'll be okay." She answered reluctantly before engulfing Rayne in a hug.

Rayne was surprised, but wrapped her arms around her for a comforting hug. "Just give me some time Lark to work my feelings out." Rayne whispered in her ear causing the knot in Lark's stomach to tighten, kissing Lark's cheek lightly.

Lark stood up with her head down unable to look at Rayne and headed for the door wiping away her tears before disappearing with Rayne watching her leave.

VI

"Hey, Tom!" Rayne shouted towards the door and watched as he entered.

"Yeah." He responded when walked into the room confused as to why Lark walked out of the room crying and stood at the end of the hall near the elevators talking to Elaine who had just stepped off the elevator.

"I need you to do me a favor by taking Lark back to the hotel and make sure she gets there safely, please." Rayne asked, knowing she could trust him with Lark's safety.

"Sure, no problem." He answered with a smile and glad for the opportunity to have a celebrity in his car.

"Listen, you need to sneak her out though because check out the front of the hospital with all of the reporters." Rayne informed him, pointing to the TV as the news was still on showing the reporters.

"Holy shit!" He answered with shock at the amount of reporters camped out front. "Alright, I should be able to get her out without incident because I'm parked in the garage basement." He answered reassuringly.

"Great! I really appreciate it. Hey, where has Danielle been? I wanted to thank her for saving my life."

"Well, Director Cady isn't too pleased with the way she handled her team at the house." He explained.

"How do you mean?" Rayne asked confused.

"She took a kill now discuss later attitude when she entered with her team. We could have contained all of them without any bloodshed and kept you from getting hurt, but she went in like gangbusters!" He informed Rayne disgusted by Danielle's actions.

"That is totally off the wall for her. I can't believe it." Rayne answered with total disbelief as to what Tom had just told her about Danielle.

"Listen, I'll head out with Lark. Take it easy and I hope to see your sorry butt up and around soon." He teased with a laugh as he left the room.

"Thanks." Rayne answered as her voice trailed off and she laid her head back against the bed wondering what was going on with Danielle.

Tom joined the two women at the end of the hall. "Oh, Elaine, this is Tom he's a Secret Service Agent that will be escorting me back to the hotel."

"Hello Tom. I'm glad you'll be helping Lark get out of here. Do you think we'll be able to get her out of here without incident?" Elaine asked as she shook his hand.

"Shouldn't be a problem. I'm parked in the garage basement and my windows are tinted very dark so, we should get out without them knowing she's there." He answered confidently.

"Okay, great. I'll leave my car where it is and ride with you both so, the reporters think that you're still here at the hospital. Let's just hope that there isn't a lot of reporters at the hotel." Elaine explained the plans as they stepped on the elevator.

"If there are reporters we can arrange to go in the back way unnoticed. I'll call the hotel once we get there and see what the scene looks like first." Tom explained as the elevator stopped at the basement and he stepped off first. "Perfect, no one's out here. Come on ladies it's safe." He answered waving them off the elevator as they hurried to his car.

Rayne's thoughts of Danielle didn't last long and a certain green eyed, blonde woman replaced them. *'Come on Rayne collect your thoughts and emotions. How do I get past what happened between us?'* She wondered as the orderlies entered the room to take her down for another CAT scan.

Rayne spent about forty-five minutes at the CAT scan and returned to her room to find her brother Shayan waiting for her. "Hey, babe. How are you feeling?" He asked concerned walking to her bed and kissed her forehead.

"I'm doing a lot better, thanks. I hope you're here to spring me from this joint." Rayne answered with a laugh.

"Let's hope so, the doctor said he would be in shortly."

"Great! Please tell me you brought some clothes for me?" She asked with a smile and a wiggle of her eyebrows.

"No, I didn't. I thought you wanted to walk out of here in that fashionable, breezy in the back hospital gown." He teased with a laugh.

"Oh, yeah. These are such the fashion statement aren't they?" She asked with a laugh, as she looked the gown over.

"Well, I have the test results Miss Donovan and you'll be happy to know you do have a brain." The doctor teasingly laughed when he entered the room and walked towards the bed.

"We always wondered if she had one and now it's confirmed that she does my parents would be so happy to know that." Shayan sarcastically replied and received a strong punch in the arm from Rayne as everyone laughed.

"What is this a hospital or a comedy club?" Rayne asked humorously.

"Well, now that we've established you have a brain it's perfectly fine. No problems, no bleeding nothing." The doctor advised her.

"Oh, mom and dad will be so pleased to know they were wrong all these years and there isn't anything wrong with you." Shayan laughed harder as Rayne pinched his neck and held it much to his protest.

He tried to swat her hand away while he laughed. "Knock it off Rayne you're going to give me a hickey."

She let go of his neck and pushed him away. "You're such a jerk." Rayne teased with a laugh. "So, doctor I can go right?" Rayne asked hopeful and looked up at him while he documented her chart.

"Yes ma'am you may leave seeing as how we found no evidence of a skull fracture or residual bleeding which we were worried about. Take it easy for the next couple of days and follow up with me for a recheck to be on the safe side. You'll have to have the stitches removed in about a week." He advised with a smile and left the room.

"Sounds great!" Rayne answered tossing the covers off and sat up as Shayan handed her the clothes he brought for her. He stepped away from the bed and closed the curtain as Rayne stood to dress. She felt slightly off balance, but regained it after a few minutes and dressed quickly as she was eager to get out of the hospital.

She slipped on a pair of Sperry Docksiders that Shayan had purchased for her along with shorts and a t-shirt. He knew he didn't dare purchase jeans as Rayne hated to wear pants unless absolutely necessary. She opened the curtain to find the transport tech waiting with a wheelchair to escort her out.

"Oh, no way!" Rayne protested as Shayan laughed and pointed to the wheelchair to get in.

"Sorry, hospital policy ma'am." The tech advised her.

"The hospital and the wheelchair can bite me!" Rayne answered with angered sarcasm and climbed in the wheelchair reluctantly, rolling her eyes towards her brother's taunting with a sneer.

The transport tech wheeled her down the hall and stopped at the desk to get her discharge papers to sign. Rayne looked around and back to her brother mischievously as she spied another wheelchair. "Hey, Shay! Get in that one and let's race like they did in the movie 'Days of Thunder.' She mischievously coaxed her brother.

"No, you behave." He objected and warned while pointing at her to get his point across.

"You're no fun anymore now that you've gotten old." Rayne teasingly laughed and shied away from her brother who attempted to pinch her ear. "No, don't hurt me I'm injured." She jokingly whined loudly, getting a laugh out of her brother.

"We need you to sign your discharge papers Miss Donovan." The nurse commented and handed her the paperwork. Rayne signed the paperwork and the transport tech delivered her to Shayan's rental car. She got in and leaned her head back on the seat, as she still felt a little woozy.

"You okay?" Her brother asked with concern as he slipped into the driver's seat.

"Yeah, I'll be fine. I just need to get my balance back to normal is all thanks for asking." She smiled reassuringly and leaned her head against her hand, which rested against the car door.

"So, what's up with Lark?" He asked knowing Rayne was avoiding talking about her.

"I told her I needed more time to figure out whether I would be able to forgive her and if I could look at her in any other way than seeing betrayal." She replied, looking at him then back out the window.

Rayne thought back to the night of their anniversary and relived all those feelings of hurt, deceit and betrayal once again. Her blue eyes filled with tears as she looked out the window and calmed when she saw the turquoise colored ocean, which filled her with a feeling of peace and calm.

She loved the ocean and all of it's beauty, power and tranquility she fondly smiled knowing she would be spending time experiencing the oceans majestic powers by hanging out at her parents beach house. "Rayne." Shayan replied and touched her arm to get her attention.

She was snapped out of her happy thoughts and she turned to him. "Huh?"

"I asked what are you going to do?" He repeated his question.

"I'm not sure. Listen, can we just not talk about this please. My head already hurts enough." She asked and rubbed her forehead pretending her head hurt when in fact, she just wanted to end the line of questions.

"Sure, no problem." Shayan answered knowing the questions towards her situation made her feel uneasy. "I'm here if you need to talk okay?"

"Thanks Shay-Shay." Rayne answered with a grateful smile that her brother cared so much for her; calling him by the childhood name she had given him.

"No prob Gooniebird." He teased and flashed her a wink with a mischievous smile when she turned to him with a raised eyebrow letting him know that the childhood name he gave her was not very pleasing to her.

She mockingly laughed and looked back out over the ocean with a peaceful feeling for once in the last six months. Shayan pulled the car up to the beachfront home their parents owned and that they vacationed at every year. Rayne chuckled with happiness when she saw Brandon and Cole waiting on the front steps for them to arrive.

"There are my boys waiting for me." Rayne replied affectionately with an adoring smile.

"Yep, they have been worried about their Auntie Rayne." He chuckled and put the car in park then turned off the ignition.

Rayne opened the car door and was met by two very anxious and out of breath boys who engulfed her in a hug the minute the car door opened. "Hey guys!" Rayne excitedly greeted, looking down at them.

"Auntie Rayne, are you okay?" Brandon asked with concern, as he looked her over.

"Yes, I'm fine. I promise." Rayne reassuringly smiled, to remove the look of concern from their cute little faces.

"We were so worried when daddy told us you were hurt." Cole admitted and hugged her neck tightly again.

Rayne smiled and thought about how wonderful it felt to have her nephew in her arms. She came very close to never feeling that ever again which scared her. There was nothing more wonderful in the world than to be loved unconditionally and that's what her nephews gave her, unconditional love. Her eyes watered at the thought as she held him tighter and kissed his cheek.

139

"You were just worried we wouldn't make our fishing trip. I know how you two are!" Rayne teased and tickled him, causing him to giggle hysterically. She stopped tickling him and both stared at her with huge smiles.

"We really were worried about you because we love you Auntie Rayne." Brandon informed her and both hugged her.

She smiled and hugged them tighter before placing a kiss on each one's cheek. "I love you both very much too."

"Come on boys. Let's get Auntie Rayne in the house." Shayan suggested with a laugh as the boys held each of Rayne's hands to escort her to the house.

Holly met everyone at the door with a smile and engulfed Rayne in a hug. "Hey, sexy. How you feeling?" She asked teasingly yet with concern.

"A lot better thanks." Rayne answered and hugged her tighter, happy that she was with loved one's. She broke her hug and leaned down to Holly's expanded abdomen. Rayne placed her hand on her stomach. "How's my favorite niece?" She asked with a smile and felt the baby move under her hand. Rayne laughed proudly as she stood up. "She loves her Auntie." Rayne exclaimed with a laugh as everyone joined in on it.

"Who doesn't?" Holly chuckled as everyone headed into the living room.

"Well, you two, tubby time." Shayan ordered and pointed to the boys who sighed disappointedly.

"Come on dad! We want to stay with Auntie Rayne." Brandon whined.

"Hey, I'm not going anywhere. Go take a tubby and then we'll play some games before bed, okay?" Rayne suggested and swatted their butts to get them moving.

"Yes!" Cole excitedly shouted as they ran for the bathroom with Shayan in tow to start the water for them.

"Hey, is Shay-Shay going to take a tubby too?" Rayne teased her brother as he turned and gave her the finger with a laugh. "Ooh that hurt!" Rayne sarcastically countered with a laugh.

Holly wondered if Rayne really felt as good as she let on. *'I don't know how she could considering the beating she took which shows on that beautiful face of hers.'* Holly thought sadly and with concern as she watched Rayne fix something to drink noticing the black eye, bruised cheek, swollen nose, and the split lip she possessed.

"Rayne are you sure you're okay?" She asked concerned, and walked over to Rayne.

"Physically or emotionally?" Rayne asked with a nervous laugh and glanced back at Holly then down to her drink.

"How about both?" Holly asked with a warm smile, hoping she would open up and tell her what was going on.

"Well, physically I'm feeling really sore. Emotionally I feel completely torn." She answered reluctant to talk about her feelings and turned to the window, looking out over the Pacific Ocean.

Holly placed her hand on Rayne's shoulder and stood next to Rayne, who turned and looked at her. "Talk to me is it Lark?" Holly asked softly, knowing that was what was bothering Rayne, but thought she'd give her the chance to talk her feelings out if she wanted to.

"As always." Rayne answered with a chuckle and looked back out the window.

"Do you want her back?" Holly asked knowing this line of questioning was hard for Rayne. Holly remembered how difficult it was to get Rayne to open up and talk about her feelings when she left Lark before.

Rayne inhaled deeply fighting what her head told her to do and what her heart wanted. "Well, I do, but I don't know how I can get past the feelings of hurt and betrayal I feel when I look at her Holly." Rayne answered sadly and looked at her sister-in-law. She was grateful to have her in her life as she considered Holly the sister she never had. She knew she could talk to her brothers about certain things, but sisterly chats were different.

"Rayne, I know you still love Lark and the two of you are meant to be together. She hurt you terribly and you have to find out whether your life is happier with or without her despite everything that happened."

"Yes, I do." Rayne confided with a slight smirk, still conflicted about how she was going to get past her feelings.

"I'm sure you're going to figure a way out and you'll find that your life will be much happier with her in it." Holly implied and walked away, leaving Rayne with that thought.

Rayne exited the house and walked down to the beach, inhaling the fresh ocean air as the cool Pacific breeze caressed her face. She sat out on the rocks and watched with amazement at the ocean's beauty as the waves pounded the shore. Rayne thought about Lark and how much she loved her. She figured she might feel differently towards Lark if she accepted responsibility for her actions instead of acting like she was no part of it. Rayne stayed on the beach for a little while longer and headed back to the house as she was tired of going over the same thing so many times. She wanted to play games with the kids and not think about so much serious stuff at the moment, she needed a break.

Rayne spent the remainder of the evening playing games with the kids before tucking them into bed and telling them a bedtime story. She watched the two boys sleep peacefully and smiled lovingly. She thought about the time her and Lark talked about having children.

They fought over who they wanted the kids to look like and of course, Rayne wanted them to look like Lark which Lark wanted no part of and vice versa. Rayne smiled at the fond memory and inhaled deeply to calm the tightness she felt in her throat. She desperately tried to fight the tears that formed as her emotions began to take over. *'Well, at least children, our children weren't involved in this whole mess. It was difficult enough for the boys when we broke up. I can't imagine how devastating it would have been for our children if we had them.'* Rayne thought sadly, leaning down to kiss Brandon's forehead and then did the same to Cole. She smiled proudly as she glanced back at them and turned on their night-light before heading out of the bedroom for her own.

Rayne opened the windows to hear the roar of the ocean, which allowed her to sleep peacefully, and crawled under the covers for some much needed rest. She laid thinking about her life with Lark before everything happened and remembered how she felt so alive and happy with Lark in her life. She had always told her they could work out even the toughest problems; actually they had made a promise to always do that, something that Rayne had forgotten until just then. *'How can I make a promise like that and go back on it? I love Lark and I want to share my life with her despite everything. Maybe if we just talk everything out I can get past these feelings of betrayal.'* She thought with renewed hope and picked up the phone, dialing the number to Lark's hotel suite with no answer. *'That's strange. Maybe she went to bed early.'* Rayne reasoned and dialed Lark's cell phone with no luck there either. She clicked the phone off and closed her eyes to drift off to sleep. *'I'll try to catch her tomorrow.'* Rayne thought as Morpheus took her to her dreams.

Rayne woke the next morning to a tickle under her nose and grabbed the hand, which held the culprit, a feather. She opened her eyes expecting to see a nephew but instead, found her baby brother Jayce sitting next to her with a mischievous grin. "Jayce!" She happily exclaimed and sat up in bed, hugging him.

"Hey, sis! It's about time you woke up!" He answered with a laugh and broke the hug to look at his sister. "You got worked over pretty good. Is the other guy dead?" He chuckled.

"Yep." She answered with a laugh.

"Figures as much. No one messes with my sis and gets away with it!" He proudly laughed. "I'm glad you're okay though."

"I told you I was fine, but as usual you didn't listen to me." She answered flashing a sarcastic grin and punched him in the arm.

"Since when haven't I listened to you?" He asked teasingly.

"Since your entire life! Case in point when I taught you to hang upside down on the parallel bars and I told you not to take your leg off. But you didn't listen and you had to remove your leg to show off and fell down breaking your elbow. Then guess who got blamed ME! Why?" Rayne asked tauntingly.

"Okay, okay you made your point. You! You got in trouble." He answered with a sheepish grin.

"That's right, me! I still haven't gotten over the fact that I couldn't ride my bike for a month and I had to do all of your chores!" She informed him with a laugh and poked her finger in his chest.

"Okay, I owe you some pampering. So, get your ass out of bed and let's go fishing with the boys. I'll get your breakfast for you while you dress." Jayce offered with a chuckle and stood up, heading towards the door.

"Dude, you read my mind." Rayne answered with a grin and climbed out of bed to dress as her brother chuckled, closing the door behind him.

Lark was awake most of the night, which was very unusual for her. Her thoughts were on a certain dark-haired beauty with exquisite blue eyes. Lark had gone down to the hotel bar staying until it closed to try and keep her mind off of Rayne, but couldn't do it. She had a nervous tension about her from worry that Rayne would not be able to forgive her. Lark also couldn't believe that Hazel was the insider. She had a better sense of betrayal now and knew a little bit about what Rayne felt when she betrayed her. *'It hurts like hell.'* She thought and was glad that Hazel wasn't her lover because she wouldn't have been able to handle it.

Lark was amazed that Rayne was able to do it so well, but then again her name is true to form, which means mighty. *'I can't believe I hurt her like that.'* Lark thought, disenchanted with her actions as the phone interrupted her thoughts.

She quickly picked up the phone hoping it was Rayne, but was disappointed to find that it was Elaine. "Lark, don't forget you have the awards show tonight and the autograph session at the convention center this afternoon."

"I'm sorry Elaine. You'll have to cancel the autograph session and I don't think I can make it to the awards show tonight either." Lark informed her as she just didn't feel like going to either, plus she wanted to talk to Hazel to find out what happened.

"Okay, aah I can cancel the autograph session, but you really must attend the award show. I mean you're up for an award Lark." She emphasized her point.

"Alright, I'll go to the award show if you clear my schedule for the next five days."

"Wait, what's going on? Where are you going?" She asked nervously and wondered how she was going to clear her schedule without pissing anyone off.

"I'm going to Greece. I have to get away and there's no negotiation on this one Elaine, understood?" Lark told firmly. She loved vacationing in Greece and it was one of her favorite places to visit with Rayne. They had a wonderful time there together and their trips there always held a special place in her heart. She hoped going back would make her feel like she did when she first visited the country with Rayne.

Elaine knew that Lark had good reason to cancel the engagements considering what she went through and didn't press the issue, as it was the first time she had ever cancelled any event. "Okay, fine. I'll make the arrangements and have the courier bring over your ticket. When do you want to leave?"

"Tomorrow and I need two tickets." Lark informed her.

"Is Rayne going?" She asked excitedly.

"I hope so." Lark answered reluctantly, as she wasn't sure if Rayne would accept the trip or not.

"Me too. I'll have everything taken care of and have them sent over to you within the next hour. Don't forget you start filming the day after you return." She reminded Lark of her shooting schedule for her new movie.

"Yes ma'am and thank you." Lark answered sarcastically and clicked the phone off.

Lark went to put the phone down and it rang again. "Hello." Lark answered when she clicked the phone on and held it to her ear.

"How's my baby girl?" Lark's father asked with happiness in his voice to hear from his daughter.

"I'm okay daddy." Lark answered undecidedly.

146

"You don't sound like it baby. What's going on and why didn't you call me last night? I had to find everything out by calling Director Cady." He asked, slightly irritated that his daughter didn't call him and he was worried.

"I'm sorry. I just had a lot of things on my mind. Rayne was injured very badly and I just wasn't thinking very clearly. I told Elaine to call you, but she must not have gotten through to you and mom." Lark explained.

"Your mother and I were very worried. How is Rayne doing?" He asked with concern.

"She's a lot better now and she's at the beach house with her family."

"Why aren't you with her? Has she not forgiven you?"

"She asked me to give her time to work through her feelings so, that's what I'm doing." Lark explained as the tears rolled down her cheeks at the thought of not being with Rayne right now.

"Well, respect her wishes and I'm positive everything will work out for you both." He reassuringly answered, confident that they would be a couple again very soon.

"I hope so daddy because I love her so much."

"I know you do princess. Now, believe what your old man is telling you. You two will be back together again, okay?" He answered with a chuckle.

"Okay, daddy." Lark answered with a laugh.

"Your mother said to tell you hello and you hang in there baby."

"Tell her I said hello and I'll be in Greece for about five days so, I'll call you both when I get there."

"Okay, you have a safe trip and remember what I said about Rayne. I love you sweetheart."

"I love you too daddy and give mom a kiss for me." Lark answered with a smile.

"I'll do that. Bye sweetie." He replied and ended the conversation.

"Bye daddy." She answered feeling more confidant and assured as she clicked off the phone and headed towards the shower.

Lark finished her shower and dressed when she heard a knock on the door. She answered to find the front desk clerk delivering the airline tickets and her itinerary, which had been delivered to the hotel as Elaine said they would be.

"Thank you." Lark answered with a grateful smile.

"You're welcome Miss Morgan. Is there anything else I can do for you?" The friendly man asked.

'Yeah, stop kissing my ass!' Lark inwardly thought, as she looked the tickets over. "Yes, could you tell the limo driver I'll be ready in fifteen minutes and have someone pick up my bags please?"

"Absolutely. I can take your bags down now." He offered and grabbed her bags, heading off down the hall.

"Thank you." She called out and sat down at the desk to write Rayne a letter.

Lark called ahead to the headquarters to let Tom know she was on her way and he met her at the front door along with the photographer to fulfill her promise to him of a picture. She finished the photo session and he thanked Lark repeatedly as his

148

buddies were envious of him getting his picture with Lark. Everyone crowded around Lark for her autograph just the same.

"Now, don't crowd the lady guys. Rayne wouldn't be happy about that." Tom replied protectively towards Lark.

Lark looked up at Tom when he mentioned Rayne's name and sadly wished that were the case with Rayne. Just hearing her name made Lark's heart skip a beat and jealous that others spend time with her instead of herself being with Rayne. She wanted her all to herself and didn't want to share her tall, dark, gorgeous lover, well, former lover, *'hopefully soon to be lover again,'* Lark thought wishfully as she passed the autographed item to the fan with a slight smile.

Lark just wanted this whole terrible mess to be finished so her and Rayne could go back to sharing their hopes, dreams and lives together once again. Lark was really in no mood to be cordial or to be signing autographs, but she did promise. She wanted to make sure she kept her promise as she was grateful to everyone who helped bring her back alive from the whole terrible ordeal. *'Particularly, Rayne who I wish I could show how grateful I am in so many different ways.'* She thought and handed the last item back. "Okay fellas. That's it right?" Lark asked checking to make sure she didn't forget anyone.

"Unless you count pictures?" One hopeful Secret Service Agent asked.

"Sorry guys, Tom is the only one I'm taking a picture with today." Lark answered with a smile and patted the slightly embarrassed agent on the back.

"Aah, too bad." They answered with disappointment.

"Tom, could you please take me to see Hazel?" Lark asked reluctantly as she wanted to know why she did it, but then in a way, she didn't. She figured it would be best to find out so she could move on. "Oh, Jimmy. Have that blown up for me and bring it tonight for me to autograph so, I can send it back to Tom, okay?" Lark asked her photographer.

"Sure thing Lark. See you later." He confirmed as Lark and Tom headed down the hall to the interrogation room.

Lark took a deep breath to calm her anger over Hazel's betrayal before entering the room. She entered and saw that Hazel sat with her head knelt down. "Hazel how could you?" Lark asked with disbelief as she hesitantly walked towards the table.

Hazel looked up with a slight sneer and glared at Lark. "Why did you come here Lark?" She asked sarcastically.

Lark was taken back and surprised by her sarcastic demeanor. "To find out why a trusted friend would do something like that to me?" Lark asked agitated by the woman's audacity.

"More like employee Lark. Look, don't read into it too much. I did it for the money, plain and simple." She answered back coldly.

"I can't believe you of all people would betray me Hazel. If you needed money I would have given it to you. How could you?" Lark asked in disbelief and shook her head.

"Look whose calling the kettle black Lark? It hurts to have someone betray you doesn't it? I told you. I did it for the money and I never really considered you a friend only an employer. Besides, you couldn't have offered me as much as I received from that group. So, just get out of here and stop bothering me." She demanded agitatedly and waved her hand for Lark to leave.

Lark headed to the door and opened it before turning back to Hazel. "Enjoy your money in prison." She replied callously and exited the room, running smack dab into Danielle. *'Great! Could it get any worse?'* She wondered incredulously.

"Find out what you wanted to hear?" Danielle asked with a sarcastic tone in her voice.

"Yep, that she betrayed me for money." Lark impersonally answered and attempted to walk away.

"Get used to it Lark. People do that to others all the time. You should know that most of all, because you're so good at it." Danielle snapped with sardonic anger.

Lark stopped in her tracks and turned around to face Danielle. "That's between Rayne and I Danielle, not you." Lark answered with fiery green eyes.

"It seems like Rayne doesn't want to have anything to do with you anymore." She answered with a laugh.

"Oh, bite me bitch!" Lark answered nastily and turned on her heels heading towards the front door of the building, leaving a stunned Danielle in her place.

Lark jumped into the limo and angrily slammed the door behind her before the driver could do it for her. He got in the limo and rolled the middle window down reluctant to speak to her, but knew he needed the directions. "Where to Miss Morgan?" He asked as he looked at a very agitated blonde through the rear view mirror. Lark handed him the directions to where she needed to go and sat back in the seat without saying a word. She thought it was best to say nothing because this man didn't deserve her being nasty to him.

'Who does Danielle think she is? She doesn't really think Rayne wants her does she?' She thought annoyed and then a sly grin appeared on her face when she realized that Rayne had told her she only wanted to be friends with Danielle and her anger with the woman subsided. She took out the letter she wrote to Rayne and reread it before putting it in the box she had for her and began to wrap it. *'I have got to get away from all of this negative crap before I have a nervous breakdown.'* She anxiously thought and

151

finished wrapping the package. Lark lost herself in thoughts of Rayne and whether she thought Rayne would be able to find it in her heart to forgive her. She hoped that she would and was encouraged by the way Rayne had acted the last time they were together. *'She was her loving, caring, funny self like she always has been.'* She remembered and was snapped out of her trance when the driver opened the door. "Oh, where there already?" Lark questioned surprised and raised the phone to her ear, dialing her desired number.

"Hello." The feminine chipper voice greeted on the other end.

"Hi Holly. It's Lark."

"Hey, Lark! Let me get Rayne, hold on." Holly excitedly offered.

"No, Holly please don't!" Lark exclaimed nervously to stop her.

"I don't understand. Why not?" Holly asked bewildered with her demeanor.

"I don't want to pressure her so, it's best if I don't see her. I have something to leave for her." Lark explained, as she did want to see her, but also wanted to respect her wishes. "I'm out front and I'll come in as long as she's not in the housu."

"Aah, okay. Well, she's down at the beach with the boys." Holly stammered confused with the situation.

"I'll be right in then." Lark answered and clicked the phone off, heading towards the door, followed by the limo driver who carried the baggage. Holly opened the door just as Lark approached. "Hey, Holly!" Lark replied with a smile as she hugged her.

"Hey, Lark. How are you?" She asked with concern.

152

"I could be better." She answered with a shrug of her shoulders and felt uncomfortable talking to Rayne's family about it, as she didn't want put Holly in the middle of everything.

"Oh, I brought Rayne's clothes and her computer over for her." Lark informed her and motioned to the limo driver to put the bags just inside the door.

"Oh, okay. I'm sure she'll be happy to wear her own clothes rather than Jayce's." Holly answered with a laugh.

"Jayce is here?" Lark excitedly asked. "He sure got here fast."

"Well, you know how protective the boys are of their sister." Holly answered with a laugh and a wink, motioning Lark into the kitchen.

"The feeling's mutual with Rayne towards her brothers." Lark added with a giggle, following Holly into the kitchen.

"Can I get you a drink?" Holly offered.

"Sure, how about tea?" Lark asked grateful for the cold beverage.

"Raspberry or Peach?" Holly queried and peaked her head out of the refrigerator to look at Lark for her answer.

"Hmmm, I'll take peach." Lark answered with hesitation because she loved both flavors. "How is the baby?" Lark asked, walking to the window and looked down at the beach.

"Ornery as ever." Holly answered with a shared laugh from Lark as she pulled out a glass from the cupboard.

"She sounds kind of like her Auntie Rayne." Lark laughed harder as did Holly.

"Let's hope she's not as mischievous as her auntie or I'm in big trouble because the boys are just like her." Holly chuckled.

"It must just run in the family." Lark answered back with a snicker.

Lark saw Rayne down on the beach with her two brothers and nephews. She smiled lovingly as she watched Rayne patiently help Brandon put the bait on his fishing pole. Lark's heart fluttered and her eyes watered as she gazed upon her gorgeous lover. She watched as Brandon said something to Rayne, which made her laugh and tickle her nephew who giggled. Lark caught the breath that escaped her momentarily as she loved to see Rayne's smile. It melted her heart every time Rayne flashed it.

Lark wished she were down on the beach with her right now despite the fact they were fishing. She would deal with that for the opportunity to be next to Rayne. Lark wanted to give Rayne the space she needed and didn't want to take a chance of blowing it with her so, she decided it was best to stay in the house. *'Oh, how I love her.'* Lark longingly thought and watched Rayne help Cole with his fishing pole, noticing that her face had been kissed by the sun and was tanner now. Lark envisioned their own children down there with Rayne teaching them how to fish and that she would just sit off on the side watching them, enjoying being a family. Rayne was wonderful with the children and she knew she would make an excellent mother which was a dream they shared, to have many children in their lives. *'Snap out of it Lark, that part of your life may never happen.'* She told herself firmly. She chuckled, as everyone got excited when Brandon caught a fish and reeled it in.

"Lark! Hello?" Holly replied as Lark snapped out of her reverie and turned to her.

"Huh? Sorry, Brandon caught a fish." She exclaimed with excitement and pride, pointing towards the beach.

"He did? Oh, here's your tea." Holly excitedly asked and quickly handed her the tea. "I have to get a picture. I'll be back shortly." Holly told her and grabbed the camera, heading down to the beach.

Lark watched forlornly as she felt left out of the family outing. She smiled when she noticed Rayne's sleeveless flannel shirt was unbuttoned revealing her muscular abdomen, which now had a bandage covering a portion of it and her sports bra. *'She is so damn sexy.'* Lark thought before becoming distressed at the thought of Rayne's injuries she sustained for her. She could only hope that Rayne would let her make it up to her. She watched Rayne intently, noticing that her sexy smile was back and thought about how Rayne was everything to her. Rayne was her whole life and she would do anything to have her back, but only on Rayne's terms. *'Rayne has to be the one to accept me back into her life. I don't want to force the issue and have Rayne regret her decision later.'* She thought as her tears of sadness flowed freely.

"Hey! Everyone get in the picture. I have to get this momentous occasion on film." Holly enthusiastically exclaimed as everyone put their arms around each other with the boys standing in front with Brandon holding his fish.

"We all need to be in the picture." Jayce suggested after Holly clicked that picture and everyone looked around the beach for someone to take the picture with no luck.

"Maybe Lark will take it." Holly answered and looked back towards the house waving, but couldn't see Lark.

"Lark's here?" Rayne asked with peaked interest and walked towards Holly.

"Yes, she stopped by to drop your things off." Holly informed her as Rayne hurried past her towards the house. Holly forgot that she was to keep it a secret as she watched Rayne run up the steps towards the house, regretful that she let the cat out of the bag.

'Why didn't Holly tell me Lark was here?' She wondered, agitated by the secrecy. Rayne was close to figuring out how she was going to forgive Lark and she was happy that she was there. She had gotten to a point now were she was excited to see or hear from Lark instead of regretting it. She entered the house through the back door smiling with enthusiastically.

"Lark! Hey! Where are you?" Rayne asked breathless as she searched the house with no luck before heading outside to see that she was gone. "Hmmm, that's strange." Rayne thought with bewilderment and disappointment as she was looking forward to seeing Lark. Rayne headed back into the kitchen and saw the package on the counter with her name on it and opened it. She found a handwritten note from Lark and opened it to read the letter.

VII

Rayne looked at the letter Lark had given her and opened the box which contained a portable CD player, a plane ticket, and a bag of white almond Hershey's kisses, Rayne's favorite. She chuckled when she saw the bag of her favorite candy and began to read the note.

Rayne,

I hope you're feeling better. I've been very worried. I wanted to tell you what I've been feeling for the past few days. I feel giddy at times knowing that I can be free to laugh, love and to be me as only I can be when I'm with you. I'm lucky to have a wonderful person such as you in my life and I want to apologize for my indiscretions, I'm sorry. It was very ignorant of me to put myself into that situation and I would do anything to make up for it, if you'll allow me to. All I can offer is all of myself to you and hope you can find it in your heart to forgive me and maybe one day trust me again.

I know that I hurt you more than anyone has a right too and I take full responsibility for my actions. You mean everything to me and you're my life. If I don't have your love in my heart my life is nothing. I can only hope that one day you'll allow that to happen again. I have to get away from here and I'm leaving for Greece tomorrow. I have included a ticket for you to join me if you want just as I promised if you saved me. I'll know what your decision is if you are on the plane with me tomorrow, please join me.

I love you, Lark

Rayne wiped the tears that trickled down her cheeks and clicked on the phone to call Lark's cell phone only to get the message saying the cellular customer was unavailable. Rayne called the hotel and was informed that Lark had already checked out. "Damn!" Rayne exclaimed and wondered how she was going to get in touch with Lark. She phoned Lark's agent and accountant who were unavailable to take her call. Rayne decided to try again later and pulled out the CD player, which had a note saying this song reminded Lark of Rayne, and for her to listen to it. Rayne took the CD player and a few Hershey's kisses along with the letter Lark wrote her and headed down to the beach.

"Hey Rayne!" Jayce called out and caught up to his sister, instantly seeing the look of disappointment on her face. "Did you see Lark?" He asked and put his arm on her shoulder.

"No, she had already left when I got in the house." Rayne answered dejectedly as she looked up at her brother.

"I'm sorry. Are you okay?" He asked with concern.

"Yeah, I'm just disappointed because I wanted to see her and I can't get in touch with her now. I'm going for a walk. I'll be back in a little while, thanks." Rayne answered with a small smile and tapped him on the chest to let him know she appreciated his concern before walking off down the beach.

She sat along the rocks and began to listen to the song "Close my eyes." By Jordan Knight. Rayne listened to the love song over and over again as she watched the ocean waves roll in and crash on shore. She thought about everything the song said and how perfect it described her own feelings for Lark. Rayne thought back to the talks they had in the soft sunlight and their walks in the park, as her tears flowed freely. She missed that with Lark and she wanted it back. Lark had finally told Rayne what she wanted to hear from her. What she needed to hear and all of her thoughts of betrayal and deceit escaped her. She felt as though the weight of the world had been lifted from her shoulders and all she wanted to do was hold Lark in her arms to tell her how much she loves her and to let her know that she forgives her. Rayne pretty much knew she would forgive Lark, but she needed to hear her say that she was sorry and that she accepted her responsibility in the whole situation before she was able to move on.

Rayne continued to listen to the song multiple times as she looked out over the ocean with renewed hope for her relationship with Lark. She smiled happily from her thoughts of feeling Lark in her arms and how sensual her lips felt pressed against hers. She couldn't wait to see her and hold her to tell her she was a fool to have been so ignorant to not try and work out their problems. *'I've got to see her but I can't get in touch with her.'* Rayne thought frustrated that she wasn't with Lark and headed back to the house.

Rayne entered her room and made sure everything was ready for her flight at mid-morning the next day and to call Danielle to set the record straight between the two of them.

"What's going on Rayne?" Jayce asked with concern as his sister said nothing to anyone when she quickly passed by them after entering the house.

"I'm getting the love of my life back." She answered with a smile and happiness, turning to her brother.

"So, you're taking Lark back? Are you sure that's what you want?" He asked, hoping his sister was positive that this was what she really wanted and she wasn't being hasty about her decision.

"Absolutely, I've never been so sure Jay." She answered confidently and put her clothes out on the chair for the next day. "I've always loved her and I guess I knew I could forgive her if she owned up to her actions which she has done. I don't want to be without her ever again. I was an idiot to wait this long to do this and unfortunately, all I can do is kick myself for being so dumb."

"I'm very happy for you Rayne and I hope everything works out between you two because I really like Lark a lot." He answered with a smile and hugged her. "Plus, I want you to be happy and I know Lark's the person that can do that to you." He spoke softly in her ear.

"Hey, we're going to Greece tomorrow. Do you want to come with us?" She excitedly asked as she broke the hug.

159

"Nah, I would just be in the way of your reunion." He answered waving her offer off, but really wanting to go.

"No, little brother you won't be staying with us. Just for the plane ride over and then you can stay with mom and dad." She corrected him, rolling her eyes at her brother's ignorance.

"Oh, okay." He answered sheepishly, slightly embarrassed for the misunderstanding. "Yeah, sure let me call to get a ticket and I'll let mom and dad know what's going on. Give me your flight info and I'll set it up."

"This will be so great!" Rayne enthusiastically stated and grabbed her ticket, handing it to him. "Maybe we can drag ourselves over to see you while we are there." Rayne teasingly laughed.

"Fat chance with you two. You're worse than rabbits when it comes to sex and considering you haven't been together for quite awhile well, you won't step out of that hotel room." He joked and turned to walk out then turned back to Rayne with a pouting look. "I'm so jealous. Can't you give me some of your tips on women? You know I live vicariously through you." He teased in a fake whinny voice.

Rayne laughed. "You're full of it bro. I know you have the chicks hanging off of you! How could you not? You're my brother and I taught you better than that." Rayne arrogantly answered with a sly grin as her brother laughed.

"Oh, yes. You taught me well." He jokingly laughed and wiggled his the eyebrows and dodged the pillow Rayne threw at him. Rayne laughed and was happy that her family was together and wished her parents were there with them.

Rayne picked up the phone and called Danielle to have her meet her at the beach house in an hour, which Danielle said she would and clicked the phone off to meet Rayne. Rayne inhaled deeply and exhaling, she thought about how glad she was that her life was taking a turn for the better. She hadn't felt this good in six months and the weight off her shoulders felt incredible. *'You should have done this months ago you idiot.'* She inwardly berated staring out the window and looking at the majestic ocean. *'I was too pig headed and full of anger to think rationally. I should have swallowed my pride so I wouldn't have hated Lark so much and we could have worked this out a lot sooner with less heartache.'* Rayne thought sorrowfully and was overwhelmed by her guilt.

"Hey Rayne! Danielle is here to see you." Shayan informed her when he stepped into the room.

Rayne turned and faced her brother still lost in her thoughts. "Aah, what did you say?" Rayne asked confused.

"Danielle? She's out on the back deck waiting for you." Shayan told her, trying to refresh her memory as to what he had just said to her.

Rayne looked down at her silver 'Fossil' watch, which Lark gave her for a birthday present and noted Danielle was a half hour early. "Oh, aah okay, thanks." Rayne stammered shaking off her thoughts and walked out to the back deck to see Danielle looking out over the ocean with her long, curly blond hair blowing in the wind.

She turned to see Rayne standing there and a smile swept across her face before she rushed over to Rayne. "Rayne, I was so worried." She replied breathless as Rayne held her shoulders to stop the impending kiss Danielle was about to plant on her lips. "What's going on?" She asked disappointed and confused as the smile disappeared from her face when she saw the seriousness in Rayne's blue eyes.

"Listen, Danielle. Aah, I love Lark very much and I've decided to forgive her." Rayne stammered nervously, knowing she was going to hurt her friend with what she had to say.

161

The tears welled in Danielle's hazel eyes at Rayne's declaration. "You're not serious." She asked, with a shaky tone in her voice.

"As a heart attack. I should never have let this hatred go this long. She's the only person I have ever loved completely and I should have given her another chance, but I didn't because I was so stubborn. I'm sorry if that hurts you, but that's the way I want my life, with Lark in it." Rayne explained sincerely and removed her hands from Danielle.

The tears fell from Danielle's hazel eyes and Rayne noticed the anger fill them. "I went through so much for you to be a part of my life. I love you so much and I wanted you to see Lark for who she is, someone who would hurt and betray you."

"What? What are you telling me?" Rayne asked as her anger and confusion amplified.

"I had that woman come on to Lark so you would know that she's not worthy of your love and that given the opportunity she would betray you." Danielle explained, pacing back and forth, trying to figure out what she was going to do next.

"How could you have done that to me?" Rayne shouted resentfully and moved closer to Danielle, who began to cry.

"Because I'm in love with you and I'm better for you than Lark."

"You're a sick bitch! You knew how much I loved and cared for Lark!" Rayne shouted with hurt, anger and that familiar feeling of betrayal that she knew so well, but now it was from Danielle and not Lark. She was so enraged that she paced around trying to calm her anger and sincerely wanted to wrap her hands around Danielle's neck to strangle her.

"Yes, I did know that, but I wanted to be your lover and would have done anything to have you, which I did, but you never even gave me a second look or hope for the past six months when we worked together on assignments. When we kissed the other day I felt that hope from you and I felt like all the trouble was worth it." Danielle explained and moved closer to Rayne who stepped away from her.

"Danielle WE didn't kiss! You kissed me and I thought about Lark through the entire kiss! I don't care if Lark was unfaithful anymore and I was stupid to not have forgiven her sooner, but I'm not going to make that mistake again!" Rayne vehemently shouted and turned to walk away.

"Rayne, wait!" Danielle shouted as she moved towards her.

"Why? Why should I even talk to you?" Rayne asked in disbelief and anger when she turned to Danielle.

"You love her that much to forgive her?" Danielle asked regretfully locking hazels with blues and seeing her love for Lark in them.

"Yes, she's the other half of my soul and my only regret is that I didn't forgive her before now." Rayne answered with complete sincerity.

"That's wonderful to love someone that much. I wanted to be the person you loved that much. I'm sorry Rayne." Danielle answered sadly.

"Yeah, whatever Danielle. I have to go." Rayne answered, casting aside her explanation. She didn't believe she was sorry and grew more irritated with the woman, then turned to leave again.

"There's something else you should know. Aah, she never did anything with that woman." Danielle informed her as Rayne looked at her stunned by the revelation. Rayne's heart raced and the lump in her throat formed making it difficult to breathe as her anger and guilt consumed her.

"She never?" Rayne tried to get out as her heart raced faster and the anger welled in the pit of her stomach.

"No, she refused the woman's advances despite her inebriation before passing out." Danielle explained regretfully from her actions.

"But how did she know I would be home?" Rayne asked confused regarding the other woman knowing her whereabouts.

"You told me your plans don't you remember?"

"Fuck!" Rayne exclaimed with tears filling her eyes at the thought of the pain Lark went through all those months she was away, not to mention, the guilt she carried all this time. Rayne was overwhelmingly guilty that she didn't talk to Lark sooner to find out what happened. "But I saw them naked." Rayne replied trying to sort out her thoughts and to get the whole story out of Danielle.

"That was plan beta. If she couldn't have sex with her she was to undress her and climb in bed with her until you got home to make you believe they had sex, which you did." Danielle explained as the anger raged within Rayne.

"Danielle, you need to leave before I throw you over the edge of that railing!" Rayne yelled as her face turned red from her hurt and anger while pointing at the railing of the deck.

"But Rayne." Danielle tried to say.

"Now!" Rayne shouted and moved to grab Danielle, but was stopped by Jayce who grabbed Rayne in a bear hug for fear of what she might do to Danielle as Rayne struggled to get away from him.

"Danielle, you need to leave." Shayan ordered angrily as he stepped between Danielle and Rayne, who continued to struggle and break free from her brother to ring Danielle's neck. He put his hand on her arm and pushed her along, escorting her away from the house.

Jayce relaxed his hold on Rayne and moved around to face her. "Are you okay?" He asked, seeing the hurt in his sister's mirrored eyes.

"I'm really pissed, hurt and I feel extremely guilty." Rayne answered in an incensed raised voice.

"Tell me what happened." He replied calmly to settle his fiery sister down.

"She had that bitch set Lark up so I would find her in bed with another woman because she's in love with me." Rayne explained pacing the deck and shaking her arms trying to calm her anger and guilt for being so gullible to fall for something like that. "I am so stupid Jay. How could I have done that to Lark?" She asked agitated by the situation as she looked at him with hurtful blue eyes.

"Rayne, you didn't do anything to Lark. This is all of Danielle's doings. Not yours and not Lark's. You can't blame yourself."

"I am to blame Jayce! Danielle was a part of my life and I should have known something was up with her." Rayne answered irritated and mad at herself for falling for that.

"Rayne, come on." Jayce softly answered and moved closer to Rayne, putting his arm around her. "How could you have known this would happen? You couldn't have known so stop beating yourself up about it." He tried to reassure his sister.

Rayne looked up at her brother then back down. "I should have known, but I didn't notice anything with Danielle when we worked together on previous cases. I just hope Lark forgives me."

"Lark will forgive you and you know it. Stop blaming yourself because you had no idea what was going on." Jayce told her, trying to console his sister.

"Yeah, but I shouldn't have been such an ass face all these months. I should have talked to Lark before and tried to work things out." Rayne answered sadly and with regret.

"Well, unfortunately, you let your pride get in the way, but now you have a second chance. So, don't blow it." He reminded her with a smile, tightening his hug and kissing her on the head.

"How did you become so wise little brother?" Rayne asked with a sheepish grin as she looked at him.

"I had a good teacher, you." He teased and saw a bigger smile sweep across his sister's face as Shayan ran up to join them.

"Is everything okay?" Shayan asked breathless.

"Everything's perfect bro." Jayce answered his brother with a smile.

"Hey, get in here! Lark's up for an award!" Holly shouted through the door excitedly.

Rayne's head shot up with interest and ran into the house to watch the TV. "Did you know she was up for an award?" Shayan asked as he looked at Rayne who stared intently at the TV.

"Aah no, I knew she had to attend the award show, but didn't know she would be getting one. I guess I forgot all about it with everything that happened." Rayne attempted to explain and saw Lark's picture appear on the screen, which put a proud smile on her face. Her heart raced and the butterflies in her stomach took flight from her nervousness.

"There's Auntie Lark!" Cole excitedly shouted and pointed to the TV as everyone shouted happily.

166

Rayne stood with her arms crossed chewing her fingernail nervously as the presenter opened the envelope to reveal the winner. *'Come on baby win, you deserve it.'* Rayne whispered and hoped Lark would win the award.

"The winner is." The actor announced as he opened the envelope. "Lark Morgan!" He answered enthusiastically as everyone cheered with Rayne letting out the breath she subconsciously held.

"Yes!" She exclaimed happily as Jayce and Shayan patted her on the back excitedly.

"That is so great for Lark!" Jayce replied with a smile.

"Lark looks stunning. Doesn't she?" Holly asked proudly as they watched Lark approach the podium to accept her award.

The crowd quieted and she began her speech. "I would like to thank my family, fans, producers, directors, co-stars, and my agent, but most of all I would like to thank the most important person in my life who is at home recuperating." She paused and caught her breath as it escaped her when she thought about Rayne's injuries. "I owe her my life and so much more. I love you." Lark professed softly and began to cry. She put her hand to her mouth to blow Rayne a kiss and walked off stage to a roaring applause.

Rayne stood stunned, speechless and totally amazed that Lark thanked her on national TV. She knew Lark didn't give a damn whether people accepted her or not in Hollywood because she was gay as it was a hobby to her that she happened to be very good at and if it were all gone tomorrow her world wouldn't crumble. Rayne thought about how fortunate Lark was to be treated as an equal rather than a leper. Rayne was extremely proud of Lark and wished she were there to share in her happiness as she wiped her tears away.

"That is so awesome! She thanked you Rayne!" Shayan replied elatedly and hugged his sister.

"She's awesome!" Rayne answered adoringly with a smile.

Rayne grabbed the phone to call Lark and found it to be busy. She tried for over twenty minutes to contact her with no luck. "Come on. Let's go find her." Jayce suggested with a sly grin as Rayne smiled with enthusiasm at his comment and they headed out to the car quickly.

When they reached the award show Rayne was told that Lark had just left and she may be attending the post show parties. They had no luck finding Lark at any of the parties when they stopped by them. Rayne was still unable to contact Lark by her cell phone, which was constantly busy. Rayne was bummed out that she was a Secret Service Agent and couldn't find Lark. She wanted to see her and to hold and kiss her so bad she could taste Lark's lips on her own.

"Well sis, you'll have to see her tomorrow." Jayce told her dejectedly and squeezed her shoulder for comfort as he saw the hurt in her eyes.

"Yes, it seems that way." Rayne answered disappointedly as she entered the house and headed to bed hoping the dawn would come soon so she could see her love, Lark.

Rayne tossed and turned all night with nervous tension anxiously waiting for the sun to come up. She tried numerous times to reach Lark's cell phone which she was told by the operator that the phone was having technical difficulties. Rayne had no luck reaching her agent, accountant or her family. She was finally happy dawn came and had her bags packed and in the car as she went to wake Jayce up for their trip.

Jayce wasn't too pleased at the early morning hours and headed into the shower half asleep. Rayne said her goodbye to

168

everyone as Jayce finished dressing and headed out to the car pacing around it nervously waiting for her brother. Jayce said his goodbyes and exited the house laughing when he saw his sister pacing back and forth in front of the car.

"Chill baby baby, chill!" He exclaimed with a laugh and motioned with his hand for her to calm down.

"I can't help it." She answered anxiously as she got into the car.

"Try to calm down babe. You know we have to have your coconut checked before we get to the airport." Jayce reminded her with a laugh as he stomped the accelerator and headed off down the road.

"I know. I know, I have this nervous energy that I couldn't work off with my usual exercise training because of doctor's orders so I'm keyed up!" Rayne animatedly explained and laughed when she saw her brother making faces at her.

Rayne had her follow up visit with the doctor who was still amazed at her healing powers and said she was cleared to fly, but needed to come back and have the stitches removed next week. Rayne knew she would be removing them herself rather than make the trip as they headed to the airport already behind schedule because the doctor was late.

"Damn it Jayce! I told you not to take that road!" Rayne shouted with anger and nervousness that they wouldn't make their flight.

"How was I to know there would be construction on this road?" He shouted back and looked for a way out of the traffic jam to no avail.

"We're going to miss our flight!" Rayne angrily yelled.

"Ask that officer over there coming out of the donut shop if he can give us an escort." Jayce suggested and pointed towards him.

Rayne quickly hoped out of the car and spoke with the officer, flashing her badge to ask if he could give them an escort to the airport, which he gladly agreed to. "Well, I guess it helps to know people in high places." Jayce laughed when Rayne got back in the car.

"Yes, it does." Rayne answered with a wink and a chuckle as the officer maneuvered them through the traffic.

Jayce screeched the tires to a halt in front of the rental car area. After exiting the car, Rayne unloaded the bags and thanked the officer for the escort. Jayce dropped off the keys and they threw their bags over their shoulders and headed towards the ticket checkpoint. Rayne flashed her badge and credentials for her gun as they grabbed their bags and began to run towards the gate, which of course, was all the way at the end of the concourse.

Rayne turned the corner to their gate and stopped dead in her tracks when she looked up at what she saw as Jayce slammed into her nearly knocking her to the ground. "Rayne, what in the hell are you doing?" He asked aggravated by the collision and picked up his bag that was knocked off his shoulder, looking at his sister who stood staring off in disbelief. "What's wrong?" He asked confused as he looked around and struggled with his bags.

"We're too late. The plane's gone." Rayne informed him, dejectedly staring out on the tarmac in disbelief.

"No shit?" Jayce exclaimed as he looked and didn't see the plane.

"Come on we have to catch the next one." Rayne exclaimed as they headed to the ticket counter.

"What if we can't get on the next flight?" Jayce asked breathless from the running.

"We will. I'm going to nonchalantly flash my badge and get us on the plane." Rayne answered confidently with a mischievous grin as they picked up their pace and approached the ticket counter.

Rayne flipped her wallet open when the ticket agent glanced down and saw her badge as Rayne took out her credit card. "I need to exchange these tickets for your next flight to Greece." Rayne informed her, as she handed her the tickets and her credit card.

"Yes, no problem at all." The agent cordially answered with a smile and entered their information into the computer.

"I'm going to get a drink. Do you want something?" Jayce asked as he looked at Rayne who flashed a mischievous grin regarding the availability of the flight.

"Yeah, you can get me a Dr. Pepper please, with a lot of ice!" Rayne answered.

"I should have known that's what you wanted. Isn't there anything else you drink?" He asked sarcastically.

"Sure, Mr. Pibb." She answered with a laugh and watched her brother head towards the food court shaking his head, knowing there was not much of a difference between the two beverages.

Rayne chuckled and looked back as the agent handed her the tickets. "There is an additional charge of $75 dollars per ticket for the flight change and the flight leaves in an hour out of gate A13." She informed Rayne.

"Okay, great thanks." Rayne smiled gratefully and waited for the friendly ticket agent to charge her card. She signed the receipt and grabbed the tickets before heading off to find her brother.

He approached with their drinks and a bag of food. "You owe me $150 little brother." Rayne informed him and took the drink from him.

"For what?" He asked, slightly agitated.

"For being a dummy and taking the wrong turn. They charged us a fee to change the flights." She explained as they made their way to their gate.

"Can I owe you?" He asked flashing a toothy grin.

"Dude, you already owe me now from me floating you some cash while you were in school. What do I look like? Nations bank?" Rayne sarcastically asked.

"I know, but I haven't received my monthly check yet."

"What do you spend your money on?" Rayne asked agitated with him, knowing that the amount of money they all received from their trust funds was enough to last anyone for a couple of months, but her brother was able to go through the money in a few weeks.

"Well, aah. Oh, look what I got for you your favorite." He stammered changing the subject to the white macadamia nut cookie he got Rayne and pulled it out to show her flashing her a puppy dog look.

"Oh, no little brother. Don't give me that look and you can't bribe me with a cookie, but I'll take it just the same." Rayne answered with a chuckle as she grabbed the cookie and sank her teeth into it savoring the taste of the white chocolate that she loved. "Now, back to your finances. You need to stop treating your hoochy mama's to such extravagant dinners." Rayne teasingly advised, and finished off her cookie as they proceeded to walk towards their gate.

"They are very good looking hoochy mama's though." Jayce reiterated and reveled in the vision of the sexy blonde in the extremely high cut red mini-skirt who rocked his world a few nights ago.

Rayne nudged him out of his daydream and they both laughed. "She was that hot huh?" Rayne asked quizzically and took a long sip of her favorite beverage.

"Hot is not the word Rayne. More like volcanic hot." He teased with a laugh and a gleam in his eye.

"No one is that hot except of course, my babe." Rayne answered chuckled and thought about how beautiful Lark is to her.

"Well, okay. You've got me there. So, she'd be more like a step below Lark. You are very lucky to have such an incredibly beautiful and caring woman like Lark who loves you with all of her heart." Jayce answered with envy of his sister and admiration for Lark.

Rayne smiled and looked down into her cup swirling her soda with the straw as she thought about how she lost that love that Lark has for her because of Danielle and for her own ignorance. She hoped Lark would still have that love for her. "Yes, I am very lucky and I intend to let her know that fact everyday from now on." Rayne answered with a smile.

"I hope I find someone like Lark one day."

"Well, there's only one Lark and she's unique plus she's mine, but you'll find someone to love as much as I love her. Just don't let anything come between you like what happened to us." Rayne advised him and patted his back while the announcements for first class passengers to board barked over the loud speaker. "That's us J.D. now, try to behave yourself with the flight attendants because it's a long flight." Rayne teased as she stood up and headed for the gangway followed by Jayce.

"Yeah, yeah." He mockingly answered with a laugh.

During the flight Rayne called the hotel where Lark would be staying and left a message that she was on her way. Despite the fact that she spoke perfect Greek she didn't think the front desk clerk would get the message right. *'They better give her the message right or I'll have to throw a party up on their heads.'* Rayne thought with a chuckle and agitated at the thought that the message wouldn't get through to Lark. Rayne also called her parents to let them know they were delayed and to inform them of their expected time of arrival so they could meet them at the airport.

Rayne was going stir crazy on the flight which seemed to get longer and longer. She couldn't wait to get there to see lark and this waiting was pure agony especially with her brother snoring in her ear. She contemplated sticking a smelly sock in his mouth to shut him up. Instead, she opted for a good shove of her elbow in his side snapping him out of his sleep.

"Wha...what?" He jumped in his seat and nervously asked.

"Chill Jayce. You're snoring so freaking loud the passengers can't hear the roar of the engine's." Rayne teased and casually flipped through her sports magazine.

"You woke me up for that?" He asked irritated and wiped the sleep out of his eyes.

"Yeah, I was embarrassed for you when that hot flight attendant looked at you horrified when she passed by noticing your mouth wide open and drool trickling down your chin." Rayne replied casually inwardly laughing.

"You're so full of it Rayne. I didn't drool and did she really stop by here?" He answered slightly embarrassed and agitated, as he wasn't sure if he should believe her or not.

"Okay so, the flight attendant didn't come by, but you were snoring very loud and I thought you were going to suck the wig off the elderly lady's head in front of us with your snoring. By the way, you drool!" Rayne added with a hardy laugh.

"Oh, bite me!" He snapped and shifted in his seat lying to the opposite side of Rayne to fall back to sleep.

"You better not suck your thumb either!" Rayne answered with a chuckle, flipping the page on her magazine and received a kick to the shin. She laughed harder and pulled out her portable CD player to listen to the song Lark had given her to see if it would relax her. Rayne closed her eyes and imagined she was holding her beautiful blonde lover. She imagined how soft she felt in her arms and how wonderful her lips felt pressed against her own. It only made her miss Lark more and created more pent up tension within in her.

Rayne decided to stretch her legs by walking to the back of the plane to use the head instead of the one in first class. She took her time and stretched as she waited for the vacancy sign to light up. *'These planes are too small for tall people.'* Rayne inwardly complained as her lanky body was cramped from the tight cabin, even in first class it was uncomfortable. *'Aah, maybe it's just because I want to be there already!'* She thought and ran a frustrated hand through her raven hair and sighed aggravated by the wait. *'If this person doesn't get out of the head in two seconds I think I might pull the door off the hinges and stuff them down the damn toilet!'* Rayne angrily thought as the door opened and a little elderly woman stepped out. *'Great! Nice thought there Rayne.'* She scolded and smiled, stepping out of the way to let her pass.

She finished her business and headed back to her seat to find Jayce chit chatting with the flight attendant quite candidly. Rayne stood waiting until Jayce gave the flight attendant his phone number at his parent's house in Greece. The flight attendant left and Rayne sat down snickering at her brother's pick up lines as she fastened her seat belt.

175

"What?" He asked with a chuckle.

"You've got the cheesiest pick up lines. I thought I taught you better than that." Rayne chuckled as Jayce gave her a cross look.

"I gave her my number. So, that means I'll have a date with her, doesn't it?"

"Well, she probably felt bad for you with pick up lines like that and it doesn't mean she'll call you either." Rayne teasingly laughed.

"I'll bet you $150 she calls me for a date." He suggested with a smile as his blue eyes met Rayne's.

"Oh, yeah. Bet me my own money, but I'll take that bet little brother and when you get your summer internship job you'll have to pay it all back plus interest.

"Deal." He answered with a confident smile that he would win the bet and shook Rayne's hand to seal the deal.

"Oh, and I want proof that you two go out on a date so, have dad take a picture of the both of you. You know he loves that shit." Rayne answered with a shared chuckle with her brother.

"You're tough sis." He added shaking his head and sat back in his chair.

"Hey, by the way, where are you doing your internship this year?" Rayne asked as she looked at her brother quizzically.

"I'm working at the White House." He answered with a gloating smile.

"No shit? That's great! How did you score that internship?" Rayne asked with pride and amazement.

"Well, it helps when your father is an Ambassador." He answered sarcastically with a wiggle of his dark eyebrows.

"Dad called in a favor for you?" She asked with jealousy as she pointed to him. "He didn't do that for me when I wanted an internship." She replied slightly miffed that her father didn't help her out like that.

"That's because he didn't want his little girl getting groped by the President." Jayce teased and pinched her cheek, receiving a swat on his hand from Rayne who couldn't contain her laughter.

"Yeah well, you better watch that cute behind of yours around that White House." She teased with a laugh.

"Oh, believe me I will. Listen, dad didn't call in any favors for me but I'm sure it didn't hurt that he's my father." Jayce explained, feeling it was important the she know that.

"I'm sure you got it on your good grades. What type of law do you want to do?"

"I think I'd like to do sports contracts or maybe corporate law. I'm not sure yet." He answered with a shrug of his shoulders.

"The Secret Service isn't a bad place to work." She suggested with a sly grin and looked over at her brother.

"Oh, yeah I can see that by the looks of your face." He answered with a chuckle. "Nice benefit package you got there." He teased with a shared life with his sister.

"I really enjoy doing what I do now, but I'm not going to do the covert assignments anymore. I'm going to have them assign me to work in some other desk type job or something so, I don't have to be away from Lark so much." She informed him about her choice of a new job with the Service.

"I don't understand. You graduated as valedictorian of your law class at Harvard no less and you don't want to practice law? I don't get it." Jayce asked with confusion as he looked at his sister.

"It's not what I wanted to do once I graduated. I like doing the work I do with the Secret Service because there's more action, but who knows what I'll be doing once I get reassigned. I may get bored and help you with your practice." She suggested with a grin.

"That would be so cool." Jayce answered with excitement at the thought of working with his sister that he idolized.

The pilot made her announcement to prepare for landing and the flight attendants prepared the plane. "Yes! We can finally get out of this tin can!" Rayne exclaimed with excitement as she fastened her seat belt and made sure it was secured before raising her seat into the upright position, as did Jayce in preparation for landing.

"Hey, do you think you and Lark will be able to drag yourselves out of the hotel room long enough to do some sight seeing with me?"

"I don't know what my little vixen has planned for me just yet." Rayne answered with a laugh and a wiggle of her dark eyebrows. "Hell, she doesn't even know I'm on my way. But I'll see if we can grace you with our presence." Rayne answered sarcastically and arrogantly.

"Oh, gee. I feel so honored." He teased, rolling his eyes.

"Well, you should. What are sister's for after all?" Rayne jokingly laughed, which was shared by Jayce as they felt the plane touchdown.

Rayne's heart began to race with nervousness as she realized she would soon see Lark and get everything straightened out. The nervous butterflies in her stomach went ballistic and she wanted off the plane in a bad way to see Lark. She was the first one up and ready for the doors to open so she could disembark the plane quickly.

"Down girl!" Jayce teased when he saw how fidgety and nervous his sister had become.

"Yeah, let's just get the bags and get going." She answered dryly over her shoulder to her brother.

They hurried off the plane once the door opened and saw their parents waiting for them. "Oh, my baby!" Rayne's mother exclaimed with tears in her eyes as the tall, raven-haired woman approached Rayne and engulfed her in a hug, as did her father.

"Are you okay sweetie?" Her father asked with concern as his deep blue eyes met Rayne's matching pair and looked his daughter over with concern.

"I'm fine daddy. It looks worse than it really is, honestly." Rayne reassuringly smiled as her father hugged her again.

"Hey, what about me? I'm the baby of the family you know." Jayce teased with a sad face that he was being ignored.

"Do you know that guy Rayne?" Her father asked.

"Nope, never seen him before in my life." Rayne answered coolly and put her arms around her parents as they walked away.

"Well, thanks a lot! See if I buy you any Christmas presents!" Jayce answered teasingly, but feeling slightly neglected as he started to walk towards them.

"Aah, my little boy is jealous." Their mother teased and pinched his cheek before hugging him. "How's my little boy?" She asked and slipped her arm around his waist while they walked to join Rayne and her father.

"I'm a lot better now that I'm off that plane with that dreadful sister of mine." He said loudly and teasingly towards Rayne.

She stopped and turned to her mother. "You had to have another kid didn't you? Two wasn't enough. You had to have another?" She jokingly asked.

Her parents laughed. "Well, that's because a certain princess kept demanding that we give her a little brother." Rayne's father added and kissed her forehead.

"Since when do you listen to your kids?" She asked with a laugh as they headed to baggage claim.

Jayce and his parents stood and waited for the baggage to come down the belt with Rayne pacing anxiously wondering why it was taking so long. Rayne's mother moved next to her and rubbed her back to calm her anxiety.

"Honey, calm down. You're going to make yourself sick." She suggested with worry for her daughter as she felt the tension in Rayne's muscles.

"I know, it's just that I have so much to tell Lark and to apologize for that I just want to be there already." Rayne explained, moving her hands animatedly to stress her frustrated point.

"I know honey. I'm so glad that you two are working everything out. We really love Lark." Her mother answered with a soothing smile as Rayne looked at her.

"Thanks mom. That means a lot to both of us." Rayne lovingly smiled and hugged her mother.

"Okay ladies break up the love fest it's time to go." Jayce teased with a chuckle as he and his father approached with their bags. Rayne broke the hug and grabbed her carry on bag before everyone exited the airport.

"Oh, Miss Morgan! You had a message!" The front desk clerk excitedly called out as she recognized the actress when she passed by the desk heading into the bar. Lark wasn't able to sleep and thought maybe going to the bar would take her mind off of Rayne not being on the flight.

"Aah, thank you." Lark answered appreciatively as she grabbed the note and headed towards the bar. She took a seat out on the deck overlooking the dark Mediterranean ocean and opened the note. It was a message from Rayne saying she would not be coming. She crumpled the note before tossing it on the table as the tears streamed down her face realizing Rayne's decision was made and that she was no longer going to be apart of her life.

'How could I have been so stupid to have thought that she would forgive me? This is my fault for being so damned insecure about our relationship and putting myself into that predicament.' She chastised herself and motioned for the waiter. She needed a nice stiff drink to settle her nerves and possibly dull the pain she felt. "I would like a Mind Eraser please." She ordered and watched the waiter leave to get her drink thinking that it was an appropriately named drink.

Rayne sat quietly in the back of the sport utility vehicle staring out the window at the site's lost in her thoughts of Lark. She hoped she had received her message and wondered how she would take the latest news that Danielle set the other woman up with Lark. Rayne thought she would have to be relieved to find out nothing happened between her and the other woman. Rayne wondered how things had gotten so out of hand and how much she loved Lark, but just couldn't forgive her for her supposed indiscretions when she knew that she should have. *'I should have been able to have forgiven her no matter what.'* Rayne thought with regret. *'I put her through so much hell. I can only hope that she forgives me.'* Rayne hopefully thought as her mother broke her trance when she touched her arm.

Rayne looked at her confused. "We're here honey." She replied with a comforting smile.

181

"Oh, yeah. Aah, I'll call you tomorrow okay?" Rayne stammered nervously as her heart raced with excitement.

"Good luck." Jayce replied with a smile as he looked over his shoulder and winked.

"Thanks." Rayne answered smiling, and kissed everyone before exiting the vehicle and grabbing her bags.

Rayne threw the bags over her shoulder and walked towards the entrance to the hotel and stopped. She was so nervous that her hands shook just like they did when her and Lark went out on their first date. Rayne inhaled deeply and exhaled trying to calm her anxiety, which didn't work. *'It won't subside until I see Lark.'* she thought and headed towards the door.

Rayne entered the lobby and approached the desk. "I need the room of Julia Donovan please." Rayne requested giving Lark's fake name for when she stayed at a hotel. It was a cross between Lark's mother's first name and obviously Rayne's last name. She was happy to find that the clerks spoke English and she would not have to speak Greek.

"I'll ring her suite to see if she'll allow you up. Your name please?" The clerk asked as she put the phone to her ear.

"Aah, could you just tell her that a family member is here to see her?" Rayne asked, as she wanted to surprise her.

The clerk rang the suite with no luck-reaching Lark. "I'm sorry she's not in her room."

"Okay, could you have them deliver these bags to her room while I wait until she returns?" Rayne asked and handed the bags to the other person behind the desk, wondering where Lark could be at this late hour.

"What room?" The second clerk asked the other clerk.

"Presidential suite."

"Oh, Miss Morgan's suite?" The clerk casually commented and moved the bags behind the counter.

"How do you know it's Miss Morgan's room?" Rayne questioned with confusion as to how that person knew it was she.

"I recognized her when I saw her check into the suite and I just saw her a little while ago heading into the bar after she picked up her message." The clerk explained as Rayne quickly walked towards the bar.

Rayne scanned the crowded bar with no sight of Lark until she walked around and saw her sitting out on the back deck staring out over the dark ocean with a forlorn look on her face. Rayne smiled as her nervousness and heart rate increased at the sight of Lark who had cut her long blond hair very short. *'She's so beautiful.'* Rayne thought breathless at the sight of Lark, but was disturbed by the forlorn look Lark possessed as she stared off in the distance.

Rayne had a mischievous thought and grabbed a napkin to jot a note on it and wrote left-handed so Lark wouldn't recognize her handwriting. "Waiter." Rayne replied and grabbed the waiter when he passed. She handed him the instructions as to what she wanted along with a hefty tip.

The waiter did as he was instructed and approached Lark holding out his tray, which contained the note and a penny.

Lark looked up at him confused. "Is this for me?" She asked with disbelief.

"Yes ma'am." He answered and nodded his head in acknowledgment of the question.

Lark took the shinny penny and opened the napkin to read what was written on it. *'A penny for your thoughts I'm at the bar.'* Lark was confused as to who would send her the note, but turned towards the bar to see who the mystery writer of the note was. She didn't think it was from anyone she knew because she didn't recognize the handwriting. Everyone at the bar seemed too engrossed in their conversations with others to have sent her the note. *'This really isn't a very funny joke.'* Lark thought agitated by it. She turned around and was startled by who was sitting in the chair that her back was to.

"Where you looking for me?" Rayne asked with a mischievous smile as her heart raced uncontrollably from Lark's stunning beauty.

"Is this some kind of a joke to you Rayne?" Lark angrily asked, agitated by the games she was playing.

"Huh?" Rayne asked breathless, as she was mesmerized by Lark's beauty and stunned by her reaction to her, considering it wasn't the one she expected.

"Are you here to torture me more? First, you're not on the plane and then I receive a note from the front desk saying you weren't coming. What the hell is going on with you? Do you really think it's that funny to toy with my heart like that?" Lark angrily shouted as Rayne sat flabbergasted by Lark's reaction.

The End.

Look for the sequel to Indiscretions, Commitments (posted online as AB INITIO).

Sneak Preview...

Committments
By Cruise

Rayne swallowed the lump in her throat. Her mouth closed and she composed herself enough from Lark's stunning reaction to speak. "Aah no. The note was wrong. I called from the plane to tell you I was on my way. Jayce took the wrong turn on the way to the airport and," Rayne tried to explain as she leaned forward with her arms resting on her legs and was interrupted.

"Excuse me but you're Lark Morgan right?" A woman asked nervously as Lark looked up at her.

"Aah, yes I am." Lark stammered, as she was surprised to be recognized in Greece considering she wasn't bombarded the last time she vacationed there.

"I knew it! I'm from the states and I would love it if I could get your autograph." The woman asked excitedly as Rayne sat back in the chair and sighed irritated by the intrusion.
"Sure." Lark answered with a strained smile as the woman handed her a piece of paper and a pen, which Lark, signed for her.

"Oh, thank you so much and I love your new haircut." She exclaimed with an appreciative smile.

"You're welcome and thank you." Lark answered cordially with a smile as she handed her the paper and pen back.

185

Lark looked back at Rayne who leaned forward again. "Jayce took a wrong turn and we got stuck in traffic which caused us to miss the plane." She explained.

"You seem to have problems with planes don't you?" Lark asked sarcastically.

"Listen Lark. There's so much I need to tell you." Rayne replied as she held Lark's hand. "I have a lot to..." Rayne attempted to explain and was interrupted again by a group of fans asking for Lark's autograph. Rayne had enough of the intrusions. She needed to tell Lark everything and it wasn't going to take a back seat to autograph hounds. "Look people!" Rayne snapped as she stood and continued to hold Lark's, which was trembling. "We need some time to ourselves. Lark can we please go?" Rayne asked when she looked down at Lark who saw the distress and anger in Rayne's blue eyes.

"Of course, excuse us please." Lark answered as she stood up wondering what it was that Rayne so desperately needed to tell her.

"She'll sign autographs later." Rayne offered gruffly, not relinquishing her hold of Lark's hand and led her down the deck stairs to the beach.

Rayne walked to a quiet part of the beach and turned to face Lark. She locked her blues with green's, which sparkled in the moonlight and smiled as she held Lark's face in her hands. She was incredibly nervous and her mind as well as her heart raced a mile a minute. "You are devastatingly gorgeous Lark. I absolutely love your hair." Rayne professed breathless and lovingly smiled.

"You mean to tell me you flew across the country to tell me that?" Lark asked incredulously, as she was still miffed about Rayne not being at the airport.

"No, I came here to tell you how much I love you and that I don't want to be without you ever again." Rayne answered with a smile as she searched Lark's green eyes for acceptance. Lark's heart fluttered and the tears welled in her eyes when she saw the sincerity in Rayne's blue eyes. "Lark, there's so many things that I need to tell you and they're not coming out right." Rayne explained nervously and inhaled deeply to slow her mind down that raced faster than her mouth would allow.

Lark put her hands on Rayne's arm, which calmed her and wrapped her arms around Rayne for a comforting hug. Lark could feel Rayne's racing heart as she snuggled close to her and felt Rayne's tension release. "Just settle down and tell me what you need to, okay?" Lark asked softly, rubbing Rayne's back and felt her heart slow it's beat.

Rayne inhaled a few deep breaths as she reveled being in the arms of the woman she loved so much and was reluctant to break the hug but needed to tell Lark what happened. She held both of Lark's hands and locked blues with green. "Lark, you're the fire that burns within me, the other half of my soul and you're my only desire." Rayne replied honestly as Lark smiled with happiness at what Rayne had just told her. "I'm to blame for everything baby. I should have listened to you and forgiven you. I was a pig headed fool. So, I'm asking you, no I'm begging you for forgiveness." Rayne professed passionately, dropping to one knee and looked up at Lark with cloudy blue eyes and kissed Lark's hand.

Lark's tears fell and her knees grew weak with Rayne's confession. 'She's begging for my forgiveness when I'm the one who cheated?' Lark thought confused as she ran her hand through Rayne's hair and rested her palm on Rayne's cheek. "Baby, you have no reason to ask for my forgiveness. I'm the one that needs that from you. I'm the one who, aah cheated on you." Lark answered hesitantly with difficulty saying cheated as it pained her so much to think she had done that to Rayne.

"No!" Rayne adamantly exclaimed and stood up, holding Lark's face in her hands. "No, you didn't cheat Lark." Rayne answered with a smile as she looked into confused green eyes. "You didn't do anything with that woman." She told her softly, staring deep in her eyes.

"I'm really confused Rayne. How do you know that?" Lark asked in total disbelief.

Rayne moved her hands to Lark's shoulders. "Danielle sent that chick to seduce you so I would find the two of you together and do exactly what I did, walk out on you." Rayne explained sadly and felt her heart flutter from Lark's reaction when she told her.

Lark went limp with disbelief and Rayne grasped her to hold her up. She felt as though she had been kicked in the stomach by a horse. "Why? How?" Lark stammered unable to form any other words, as she was completely stunned. "How could someone do something so horrible like that to us?" Lark asked bewildered and confused. She turned her back to Rayne trying to make some semblance of what happened to them and looked out over the ocean trying to catch her breath, her tears flowing freely.

The tears streamed down Rayne's face seeing the pain Lark felt. Lark's pain was more than she could bare and wanted to take it away. Rayne approached Lark from behind and wrapped her arms around the trembling shorter woman who collapsed into her arms, crying harder. Lark slid her hands onto Rayne's arms that held her tight and closed her eyes, reveling in how comforting her strong arms felt wrapped around her. "It's because of me Lark. Danielle wanted you out of the picture so she would have a better chance of being with me." Rayne whispered sadly and rested her cheek against Lark's head. They stood silently enjoying the closeness and calming effect it had on one another. "I'm so sorry Lark." Rayne replied softly and Lark turned to face her.

"You have nothing to be sorry about Rayne." Lark answered as she stared into regretful, cloudy blue eyes.

"Yes, I do Lark. I should have trusted you more than what I did and I should have made an attempt to talk to you to work it out, but I didn't. I can't forgive myself for being so ignorant." She answered remorsefully.

"Rayne you couldn't have known that I didn't cheat on you. I wasn't even sure of it myself." She explained sad that she was in that position by getting drunk.

"I should have had more faith in you. You would have had more faith in me. I'm sorry." Rayne answered apologetically.

"I would have reacted the same way. I would have been devastated as you were if I would have walked into our bedroom and found you in bed with a naked woman. This past week has totally blown my mind. I mean I'm so pissed that I feel like killing Danielle! Ugh!" She shouted and spat her anger and frustration out.

189

Rayne chuckled remembering the fact that she nearly did that to the vile woman. "If it wouldn't have been for Jayce and Shayan I would have killed her." Rayne admitted with a sheepish grin and a hardier laugh.

"You would have?" Lark asked surprised and giggled.

"Yeah, I was going to toss her over the deck railing." She told her with a laugh, which was shared by Lark.

"I would love to have seen that!" Lark answered still laughing.

Rayne stopped laughing and looked into Lark's eyes with a serious demeanor. "Can you forgive me for the way I treated you this past week?" Rayne asked with regretful and guilt filled eyes.

"Did you mean any of the hateful things you said to me?"

"Not one word." Rayne answered as Lark searched her blues for the truth, which she found.

"Then I forgive you as long as you forgive me for being an idiot and not trusting your love for me." Lark bargained and ran her fingers through her lover's dark hair, which blew in her face from the ocean breeze.

Rayne felt a tingling sensation and nervousness as Lark ran her fingers through her hair. "How could I not when I look into your sweet face with those beautiful green eyes that sparkle in the moonlight?" Rayne asked softly and moved closer to Lark whose lips waited in anticipation for Rayne's. "With those very sexy lips that I love to have pressed against

190

mine and to taste." Rayne added suggestively as Lark's hands moved up behind Rayne's neck, feeling Rayne's lips lightly touching hers.

"Kiss me." Lark whispered with breathless anticipation as Rayne's lips met hers for a soul-searing kiss that melted her to the core. Lark tightened her hold around Rayne's neck with Rayne slipping her arms around her drawing her body closer to her own. Lark deepened the kiss sending a rush of warmth throughout Rayne. Her stomach had a tingling, nervous sensation as if it was the first time she had ever kissed Lark. Rayne felt the heat of Lark's body and her hardened nipples pressed against her own. Her tongue slipped out of her mouth, seductively tracing the contours of Lark's lips before sliding back in for a deep, moist kiss. Lark's passion and wetness mounted, burning with desire for her lover to scoop her up in her arms and make wild, passionate love to her. "Allow me to make love to you." Rayne whispered through her kiss as her heart nervously pounded in her chest.

"You my love are always allowed." Lark answered seductively and deepened the searing kiss.

They broke the kiss breathless and locked blues with greens smiling blissfully that they were back were they belonged, in each other's arms. Rayne's want and desire for Lark escalated, staring into her eyes and seeing the longing for her that they possessed. She kissed her lightly and slipped her hand into Lark's, leading her away from the beach. Rayne had thought about making love to Lark right there on the beach, but she wanted it to be slow, sensual, passionate, special and not sandy. "So, does that mean that I can make love to you after I've had a workout and I'm really sweaty." Rayne smiled teasingly and wiggled her eyebrows

191

suggestively at the prospect of making love to Lark in any way.

"I said you were always allowed." Lark reiterated provocatively, looking up at Rayne and winking flirtatiously.

"Yeah baby." Rayne teased in a feeble attempt of an Austin Powers imitation. "You know I'll hold you to that." Rayne guaranteed and laughed.

"I'm counting on it." Lark flirtatiously answered and stopped, leaning up to kiss her tall, dark lover. She was ecstatic to have her sexy lover back and wanted to show her just how much with that one kiss.

"Ooh, baby. Your kiss is complete bliss and takes my breath every time you touch my lips." Rayne answered with a satisfied sigh and a smile. Lark blushed smiling and wrapped her arms around Rayne's neck, drawing her close for a searing kiss that touched the deepest part of Rayne's soul. "If you keep that up you'll have to perform CPR on me don't ya know?" Rayne replied teasingly flashing an alluring smile after breaking the kiss.

"Don't tease about that babe because you just don't know how scared I was when I saw you laying there with Danielle doing CPR on you. I felt so helpless and I intend to get certified so, I never feel that way again. I hope something like that never happens again." Lark answered regretfully and shivered at the memory of Rayne having CPR done to her.

"It's okay. Don't worry about it." Rayne answered reassuringly and tried downplay the incident.

"No, it's not Rayne. What if something like that would have happened when we were alone? I wouldn't have known what to do." Lark answered seriously to let Rayne know it was unacceptable that she didn't know CPR.

"Okay, I'll tell you what. My certification is expiring this month so, we'll both go together." Rayne suggested with a smile.

"It's a date." Lark answered smiling with a feeling of assurance and kissed Rayne's hand, leading her towards the stairs.

Author's Bio:

Cruise (Debbie Bathurst) has been living and working in the South Florida area for the past fifteen years. She currently lives in Lauderhill with her partner Monica and their kids Taz (cat) and Gabrielle (dog). She enjoys sports, traveling, movies, writing and creating music videos in her spare time. She was born in Jamestown, New York and grew up in Daytona Beach. She attended Lake City Community College on a softball athletic scholarship and graduated with an Associate of Arts degree in Physical Education. She played softball for Lake City Community College for two years and

in her first year they were crowned National Junior College champions. She changed her major the following year and received an Associates degree in Golf Course Operations. She worked as an assistant softball coach for Lake City Community College while earning that degree. After working in the golf course industry for four years, she decided a change was in order and applied for Physical Therapy school. She has an Associate of Science degree in Physical Therapy from Miami-Dade Community College and was an assistant softball coach there as well. She works as a Physical Therapist Assistant by day, and a published fiction writer by night. She wrote 'Paradise Found' with her co-author Stoley, which has made the Top Sellers List at Open Book. Her trilogy, Provenance, Indiscretions, and Commitments (formerly Ab Initio) are slated for publication with **LimitlessD2D Publishing**. Indiscretions will be in print May 2003. You can find these works and others she has penned at www.clububer2000.com.

Author can be contacted at: Cruise@clububer2000.com
URL: www.clububer2000.com